Henry Cabot Lodge

Certain Accepted Heroes And Other Essays

Henry Cabot Lodge

Certain Accepted Heroes And Other Essays

ISBN/EAN: 9783743382787

Manufactured in Europe, USA, Canada, Australia, Japa

Cover: Foto ©Andreas Hilbeck / pixelio.de

Manufactured and distributed by brebook publishing software (www.brebook.com)

Henry Cabot Lodge

Certain Accepted Heroes And Other Essays

CERTAIN ACCEPTED HEROES

*AND OTHER ESSAYS
IN LITERATURE AND POLITICS*

BY

HENRY CABOT LODGE

NEW YORK AND LONDON
HARPER & BROTHERS PUBLISHERS
1897

TO

MY FRIEND AND COLLEAGUE

THE HONORABLE

GEORGE FRISBIE HOAR

SENATOR FROM MASSACHUSETTS

" Statesman, yet friend to truth! of soul sincere
In action faithful, and in honor clear!
Who broke no promise, served no private end,
Who gained no title and who lost no friend."

NOTE

With the exception of the last, these essays have all been published before in different magazines and reviews. I desire to thank the editors and publishers of *Scribner's Magazine*, of the *Cosmopolitan*, and of the *North American Review* for their kind permission to reprint here the "Last Plantagenet," "As to Certain Accepted Heroes," and the essay on "Dr. Holmes."

H. C. L.

Washington, D. C., May, 1897.

CONTENTS

AS TO CERTAIN ACCEPTED HEROES

AS TO CERTAIN ACCEPTED HEROES

THERE have appeared lately some very notable prose translations of the Homeric poems; Professor Palmer's Odyssey, and the Iliad and Odyssey " done into English " by Mr. Andrew Lang, Mr. Butcher, Mr. Leaf, and Mr. Myers. These translations seem to prove the decided superiority of fine prose in giving an English version of the great Greek epics. Whatever their advantages, metre or rhyme, or both, impose such conditions upon the translator that he is inevitably forced to depart more widely from his original than if he were not so fettered. Of course, a dry and baldly literal rendering of Homer into English prose is of little value except as a labor-saving device for the school-boy. The proposition that prose is the best vehicle for translation rests necessarily on the assumption that the prose itself is of the best, and such is certainly the case in these new versions. All are the work of ripe scholars, and all have the true literary touch. The English is not only fine, but thoroughly poetic in substance if not in form. It is true they are translations, but it seems as if nothing else could be said against them. They preserve the spirit and fire of the original better than any other rendering, and they bear us along and make us feel the rush and swing of the story with a strength of which no translation in verse has hitherto shown itself capable. I confess that I rather prefer Professor Palmer, because his language is simpler, somewhat more direct, and more purely modern. The ·slightly archaic forms and occasional archaic words used by Mr. Lang and his associates do not seem a gain. More or less archaic English is practically no nearer Homer than the English of to-day, and yet it is distant from our own modes of thought and speech. The employment of archaisms seems, in fact, to contravene directly the sound rule laid down in Mr. Lang's introduction to the Odyssey, that a translation should above all things conform to the taste and speech of its day, as otherwise it falls short of its first duty, which is to make the original as simple and comprehensible as possible.

ᵥYet, after all, this is but a small point.

Where everything is so good it is invidious to grumble, or even to draw comparisons. Moreover, my purpose is not to analyze or criticise the merits or demerits of these translations, which may be said to be wholly admirable, but to set down certain impressions which have come to me, or, rather, which have been renewed and sharpened by a fresh reading of Homer. To most boys, I think, the study of Greek is a sore trial, and it is a real misfortune that the Homeric poems should be associated in their minds with the idea of a disagreeable task. At the same time, although boys do not realize the splendor of Homer's poetry, or the beauty of Homer purely as literature, the story of Odysseus, simply as a story, has to them an abiding charm despite the highly adverse circumstances under which they first encounter it. On the other hand, it puzzles most boys, I think, as it puzzled me, to understand why it was worth while to learn with great labor a language which in the Iliad, the only book we knew, was devoted to the exploits of what seemed to the boyish mind a set of not over brave savages, very inferior in all ways to such heroes of youth as Saladin and Richard of the Lion Heart, or as Uncas and Leather-Stock-

ing. The boyish insensibility to the wonder
and beauty of the poetry passes away like
many other and better things of early days,
but the boyish judgment as to the characters
portrayed in the Iliad, after many readings
and a good many years, seems to have been on
the whole correct. If it is correct, then it is
not unworthy of consideration, for it is desirable in literature and art as well as in the practical affairs of every-day life to look at things
as they really are, and to try not to be led
away either by confusions or conventions.

As literature, the Homeric poems are so
great that the world has fallen very easily into
the habit of assuming that because the poetry
is noble and beautiful the people whom it de-
picts are noble and beautiful also. This is perhaps a natural error, but it is none the less an
error, for there is no necessary connection between the merit of a literature and that of the
people it pictures to us. We make no such
mistake with modern authors. Nothing in
literature rivals Macbeth in tragic power or in
sustained splendor of thought and diction.
Some of the greatest passages in all poetry
are spoken by Macbeth, and yet no one would
think of calling him a hero or of holding him
up as a figure for after ages to admire. We

marvel at the genius which created Macbeth, but we are in no doubt as to Macbeth's character. With Homer, on the other hand, we have associated the word heroic. The age of which he wrote is the heroic age, his verse is called heroic verse, and his characters are conventionally called heroes. It is this convention which embodies the error. Homer drew men as he saw them, with all the vivid force of genius, but that fact does not make them heroes in the accepted sense any more than Shakespeare's genius makes Iago other than the villain that he was and that his creator intended him to be.

Neither is it of moment whether the work is history or fiction. It makes no difference so far as this question is concerned whether the men and women of whom Homer sang ever lived or not. They are a good deal more real and have entered far more into human life and thought than many people who undoubtedly have lived and died, and, like brave Percy, been food for worms. They have been used as types and examples; their words have become part of the speech, their deeds a portion of the history of mankind. Their very names have gone broadcast throughout the world and have been given to children without a drop of Greek blood in their veins, who in many instances very likely went through life without ever reading the exploits of their namesakes, or knowing who those namesakes were.

Such people as those whom we know in the Iliad and the Odyssey, whether they really lived once upon a time, or whether they were but the creations of the poet's brain, deserve consideration for their effect on humanity quite as much as most well-established historic characters, and are also as a rule far more interesting. Moreover, whether the heroes of the Iliad existed or not in those precise forms, they certainly existed as a society, for Homer, like all great imaginative writers of healthy mind, pictured what he saw and knew. He threw over it all the glamour of genius, but as he was a great genius he was therefore essentially true both to life and nature.

Let us look, then, at these Homeric characters in the light of historical common-sense, with Homer himself as our authority. Let us forget for a moment that they are chronicled in verse of surpassing beauty, and take only the bare facts as Homer gives them.

Before coming to details, it must be remem-

bered at the outset that these Homeric people
have been held up for generations among the
children of men not as heroes, in the technical
sense of belonging to what is called the heroic
age, but as real and lasting heroes, to be ever
imitated and admired. We need go no further for an example than to Mr. Myers's sonnet, prefixed to this very translation, in order
to find Achilles called "chivalric." Let us begin, therefore, with Achilles, greatest and most
heroic of the heroes. What are the facts
about him as Homer gives them? They are
easily obtained, for the wrath of Peleus' son
and its consequences really form the Iliad,
and, familiar as they are, I must venture to
restate them, for on these facts, plainly stated,
the case largely turns.

Achilles was admittedly the best fighter,
the strongest man, and the most important
chief among those who gathered with their
followers for the siege of Troy. On the way
thither the combined forces landed on a buc-
caneering expedition and took the city of
King Action. To Achilles in his share of the
spoils fell Briseis; to Agamemnon, Chryseis.
But the latter was the daughter of the priest
of Phœbus, and when Agamemnon refused to
give her up the sun god sent a pestilence

among the Greeks. Then Achilles insisted that Agamemnon should give up Chryseis, and the king of men agreed, but on condition that he should have Briseis by way of compensation. Thereupon followed a dispute, purely verbal and physically harmless, which is an interesting example of the dignity of this particular body of heroes. There is in it, alas, only a ha'porth of argument to an intolerable deal of personal abuse. At one stage the god-like Achilles came almost to the point of fighting, but as that was something the Homeric warriors always considered carefully, he counselled with Athene, who advised him not to fight but to revile Agamemnon—a course which Achilles pursued with the utmost good-will and success.

We discover from the conversation which ensued that in the opinion of Achilles the king of men was " shameless," " crafty," and a " dog-face," that he was a drunkard with the " heart of a deer," without " courage to arm for battle" or " to lay ambush." Agamemnon was more guarded in his language, having a wholesome fear of Achilles' superior strength, but he carried his point and got Briseis when Chryseis was returned. Thereupon Achilles retired to his tent, a movement

which by his action has become the common
metaphor for sulking, and then through his
mother's aid he obtained from Zeus the promise that he should be avenged by having the
Greeks driven and beaten by the Trojans
until they were ready to sue for his return on
his own terms. All, as we know, went as he
amiably desired. His friends and allies were
beaten and slaughtered in a series of engagements, and Achilles brought all this upon
them, and, in fact, deserted them, because a
slave girl had been taken from him. His allies evidently understood him, for they tried
to bribe him to come back by offering gold, a
form of persuasion which was perhaps judi-
cious but was certainly not heroic. The one
cry of Achilles throughout is, in fact, that he
had not received his proper share of the
plunder, and that even from what he got the
best had been taken. For a treachery so con-
siderable and so vindictive as his, the cause,
baldly stated, does not seem very noble even
in this materialistic and money-making age.

Finally the Greeks were so pushed that
Achilles permitted his dearest friend to wear
his own magic armor and lead forth the famous Myrmidons. In the ensuing fight Patroclus was killed by Hector, who got the

armor and put it on, and the news of Patroclus' fall was brought to Achilles, who was filled with rage and grief. One might suppose that, under the circumstances, this great fighter would have caught up the first weapons he could find and rushed forth to avenge his friend. Not at all. He sat him down after much fine talk and waited until his mother procured from Vulcan a new and more splendid set of impenetrable armor. Thus equipped he sallied forth, and, as might have been expected, killed without difficulty a number of unimportant persons and drove the Trojans before him. He slew all who came in his way, even those who begged for quarter—which, it must be said, all the Greeks did habitually, and apparently from preference. In the case of Lykaon, however, Achilles went a step beyond even the general pleasant custom. Lykaon not only fell at the great warrior's feet and asked for mercy, but he was totally unarmed. Achilles, rather amused at the request for quarter, butchered the defenceless boy and passed on. This was very likely a customary deed, suitable to the time and place, but abstractly it was hardly a heroic one.

At last he came to Hector, who awaited

him outside the walls. Hector sought an agreement that the victor should return the body of the vanquished in the fight, a proposition which Achilles, with the abusive words of which he had large command, declined. Hector ran three times around the walls and Achilles failed to overtake him. Then Athene appeared in the likeness of Deiphobus and persuaded Hector to stand. Achilles threw his spear without effect, and Athene returned it. Hector threw his and turned to his brother, Deiphobus, for a second, only to find that there was no one there. Then, as Shakespeare would put it, "they fight, and Hector is slain." After his victory the "chivalric" Achilles dragged Hector's body behind his chariot, proposed to give it to the dogs, slew twelve Trojan prisoners in honor of Patroclus, and finally gave up Hector's body only by the direct intervention of the gods.

This, in the driest outline, is the story of Achilles, as Homer gives it. What manner of man do the facts disclose? Simply an unusually brutal savage of colossal strength, treacherous and cruel, ready to sacrifice friends for a quarrel over the spoils, utterly devoid of generosity towards his foes, and not particularly brave.　He wore impenetrable armor; he had horses of divine origin; he knew by divine revelation that he was going to kill Hector, and he had the treacherous assistance of a goddess.　Under such conditions it required but little courage to fight a man who, at the critical moment, had no helper, human or divine.　The fight with Hector is nobly told, but, on Achilles' side at least, it was a most ignoble fight.

Men must be judged by their own age and time and by their own standards, if we would judge them with any justice.　To do otherwise would be absurd.　But it is equally absurd to hold up men of a past age as abstractly heroes because the poet of the time, writing from his own point of view, declares them to be so. To condemn Achilles because he had the morals and manners of a South Sea Islander of the time of Captain Cook, and therefore does not come up to our standards, would be highly unjust, but to treat him as a heroic figure for all after generations to admire is simple nonsense.　He was a savage, and a bad one.　Tried even by the savage code, he stands low, and to talk of him as "chivalric" is to give him qualities utterly unknown to him or any of his fellows.　As a mere fighting savage, moreover, he falls far below the Zulus who

thronged about Rorke's Drift, or the North
American Indians who cut off and destroyed British and American armies with all the
strength of centuries of civilization behind
them.

It is not fair, however, to judge a people
from an individual. Achilles was much the
worst, as Hector was much the best, of Homer's
men. Hector showed generosity and nobility
of character, and despite his running away from
Achilles, he was, on the whole, the bravest of
them all. But what is of most concern is the
race, and on this the poem gives us abundant
information. It can be easily condensed, and
is not flattering. All the chiefs, from Nestor
down, bragged and boasted vociferously to
each other and to their foes. They had no
regard for plighted faith. The Trojan Panda-
rus shot at Menelaus when it had been agreed
that Menelaus and Paris should settle the differences by single combat. Diomed and Odysseus captured Dolon, and, on promise that his
life should be spared, Dolon gave them information about the Trojan camp. Thereupon
they slew him.

Lying they regarded not only with leniency
but approbation. When Odysseus landed in
Ithaca he met Athene disguised, and, in re-

sponse to her questions, lied artfully. The goddess, revealing herself, not only praised him for his prudence, which was natural, perhaps, but for his skill in falsehood.

They were ungenerous to their foes, gave no quarter except to preserve slaves, slaughtered prisoners, and considered that it was a matter of course to give up a captured city to rapine and destruction, saving only women for slaves and concubines, with whom each chief was amply provided. All these qualities, it may be said, are to be expected among a primitive and savage people. This is undoubtedly true, and if we treat Homer's Greeks as savages, as they ought to be treated, and not as heroes, according to the conventional modern usage, the defence is complete; but then this defence, of itself, proves the case against the heroes.

Moreover, whether savages or not, in one particular these people ought to have excelled. Physical courage is the commonest virtue of men, whether savage or civilized, and in this very point the men of the Homeric poems fall short. Let us take a few examples. In the fourth book Agamemnon "drave the cowards," as if they were a recognized body, into the midst of the army, and then warned his men not to be eager to fight single-handed,

but only to assail the foe from their chariots—
which was not exactly an inspiring form of
military address.   In the thick of the combat, whenever any fresh warriors approached,
or any man of renown, the chiefs individually
would carefully consider whether to fight or
run away, which seems to have been always
an open question, although not commonly so
regarded by fighting men, especially of heroic
mould.   So Diomed, one of the best, doubted
in the fifth book.   In the eighth book they all
bolted except Nestor, who could not run away
because his horse was "foredone," and Diomed, who took occasion, with great justice under the circumstances, to call Odysseus a cow-
ard.   Subsequently Diomed had another fit of
doubting as to whether flight was not best, but
managed, after much hesitation, to stand his
ground.   In the ninth book, the king of men
was all for taking to the ships and running
away, because they had met with a reverse.
Odysseus also doubts in the eleventh book,
and so it goes.   Examples might be multiplied
to show that flight was always a reasonable
alternative, duly considered even in the heat
of battle, and in no case a disgrace.   It is curious also to note how little hand-to-hand fighting there is.   Nearly all the death-blows and

2

wounds are given with hurled spears or with
arrows.   It is obvious that the men of Homer
had not, as a rule, any liking for close work with
the sword—the surest sign that they were not a
hard-fighting race and that they could not stand
punishment.   They evidently did not comprehend the maxim laid down by Dr. Holmes,
when he compared the American bowie-knife
with the Roman sword, that the people who
shorten their swords lengthen their boundaries.

Most striking of all, however, is the way in
which Homer's men left the field if they were
wounded.   When Agamemnon was hurt in
the forearm and Diomed in the foot, both left
the battle and betook themselves at once to
their tents.   It is not easy to understand how
any army could have done very effective
fighting when their chiefs were ready to re-
tire for such trifling hurts as these.   But it
was apparently the usual practice; and far
more significant than the act itself is the fact
that the poet treats these withdrawals from
the field as wholly a matter of course.

It would be unfair perhaps to contrast such
performances as these with the Roman fighting, or with that of the English who fell
around Harold, at Hastings, or of the Scotch
who died by the side of James, at Flodden,

or of the Americans who were killed to the last man at the Alamo without even leaving a messenger of death, as the Greeks did at Thermopylæ. It is quite fair, however, to compare these Homeric warriors with those of another primitive people also celebrated in the verse of an early minstrel. What a poor figure do the Greeks cut by the side of the Nibelungs! At the crossing of the river Hagan is struck down twice from behind, but he rises, hurt as he is, slays the boatman, and takes the boat. If he had been like Agamemnon he would have retreated to his tent and had his head bound up. Or take the most famous scene of all in the German epic, the final struggle in Etzel's hall. That grim fighting was simply impossible to such men as Homer described. In a word, the Nibelungs are as superior to the Greeks as fighters as the Iliad and Odyssey are superior to the Nibelungenlied as poetry.

Take, again, another example from a kindred race, the Jomsborg viking, who in fierce sea-fight having cleft his enemy, Thorstein, to the waist, has both hands cut off at the wrist, and thus finds himself helpless and surrounded by foes. Clasping his two boxes of treasure with his bleeding stumps he calls his few surviving men to follow him, and plunges into the sea, leaving to his enemies only a bloody wreck.   Still another instance from the same early literature of a primitive people is the familiar story of Gizli, the outlaw.   Trapped and surrounded by a band of fifteen men as brave as himself, he kills or mortally wounds eight of them, and when pierced with spears he manages to bind his cloak about his wounds, and throwing himself upon his assailants kills one more and falls dead upon the body of his foe. These men were pirates and savages, if you will, and so were the Homeric Greeks, but the Norse viking and the Icelandic outlaw were redeemed by a fierce courage and a capacity for desperate fighting of which the Iliad shows no trace.

Historically, and as a plain matter of fact, the Homeric Greeks were a number of small tribes under different chiefs, united for the purpose of destroying another, and probably kindred, collection of similar tribes.   They were primarily buccaneers, not differing in any essential respect from Morgan and the other heroes of the Spanish Main, except that they were very inferior in fight.   When faring over the sea they would land and attack any peaceful city they could get at.   Sometimes they were successful, as in the case of the holy city of King Aetion, sometimes they were repulsed, as Odysseus was by the Kebriones. In this aspect they were simple pirates. When they took a city, as has been said, they sacked it, killed the men, and carried off the women and children into concubinage and slavery. They did not, indeed, always stop there, for, in the case of Troy, Agamemnon reminds Menelaus in one passage that they are to kill every one, even to the child in the mother's womb.

When they were all gathered before Troy they quarrelled among themselves, and were eaten up by bitter feuds and jealousies. They did a great deal of declaiming, and although the language put into their mouths by Homer is magnificent, their sentiments were low, and the frequency and violence of their vituperation were amazing. They did a good deal of not very desperate fighting, were ready to run away on slight provocation, and finally carried the city by a trick. The gods, who represented their ideals, were on the whole lower than their worshippers, by whom they were at times even beaten in battle. In a word, the Homeric poems describe to us the doings of certain primitive tribes who were cruel and

treacherous, subtle and cunning, liars and brag-
garts, and, withal, not over brave, although
fighting was their principal business in life,
and courage should have been their conspicuous and redeeming quality.

Homer drew men and society as they were,
and the facts of history fall in with his facts.
It is only when we adopt the "chivalric" and
heroic theory that history and Homer fail to
agree.   Of the early exploits of the Greek
race Thucydides says: "It is impossible to
speak with certainty of what is so remote, but
from all that we can really investigate I should
say that they were no very great things."
The Greeks of history were the true descendants of Homer's men, but bore no relation to
the fictitious beings whom a late posterity has
seen fit to find in the Iliad.   The historic
Greeks as they became civilized improved in
sentiments, morals, and manners over the Homeric Greeks.   They were ingenious, subtle,
clever.   They were fertile in orators, writers,
and artists.   They produced a sculpture and an
architecture which have never been equalled,
and a literature which stands among the foremost of the world.   They have had more effect upon human thought probably than any
people who have ever lived.   They improved,

too, in fighting, but as we have only their own story, and as they retained their ancestors' habit of speaking extremely well of their own exploits, it is difficult to say how much they had improved. They fought better than the Asiatics, and they kept the Persians out of Europe, but I confess I have always longed to have a Persian account of those wars, in order to gain some means of knowing just how much the Greeks lied about the numbers of Xerxes' army.

But, after all is said, the fact remains that the Greeks politically continued to be at bottom a set of jarring, jealous tribes. They built cities, but not empires; they founded municipalities, but not states. They failed not merely to govern others, but themselves. When they came in contact with a real fighting people like the Macedonians they went down before them, and they fell an easy prey to the Romans. They were far cleverer than their conquerors, and yet, as Bagehot says: "The Romans were prætors and the Greeks barbers."

Such a fate must have been predicted for the descendants of the Homeric people if they are looked at rightly, and not through the mist of modern misconceptions. With

all their talent and all their genius the Greeks
were not a fighting or governing race.   Lowell says, somewhere, "I cannot help sympa-
thizing with the Romans, who thought it
better to found an empire than to build an
epic or carve a statue," and this sympathy
is wholesome and sound.   It is true that we
respect more for their character and force the
men who formed the Roman law and built
the Roman roads than we do those who
reared the Parthenon or produced the literature of Greece.   The Romans were statesmen, lawgivers, and soldiers, while the Greeks
ministered to their pleasure, gave them their
art, and improved their literature.   In the ancient world these different qualities did not
exist in the same nation, and it has been reserved to the English - speaking people to
combine the force and power of a governing
and conquering race with the greatest literature, excepting the Greek alone, that the
world has yet seen.

The accepted view of Homer's chiefs, however, is but part of the conventional and traditional theory about the classics generally.
The classics were indissolubly associated in
men's minds with the revival of learning and
the escape of civilized man from the darkness

of the Middle Ages. People felt for the literature and history of Greece and Rome not
only a just admiration but a profound gratitude. Thus it came to pass very naturally
that education in its highest form meant classical education. To know the classics was to
have a liberal education, the education of a
gentleman. An Englishman might be igno-
rant of the most familiar facts of science or
history either of his own or other nations if
he could quote Horace aptly and correctly.
To this day, writing Latin verses is a principal
exercise of English school-boys—a form of education about as useful and deserving of the
name as it would be to teach them to make
Choctaw acrostics or to write the Lord's
Prayer or the Ten Commandments within
the compass of the little-finger nail.

Of late years there has been a revulsion
everywhere against the classical tradition, and
the danger now is that it will go too far.
Simply because the dead languages have no
obvious practical use, it would be narrow in
the extreme to lay them aside in our higher
education. But they should stand on a true
and not on a false ground. Latin and Greek
should be studied and learned, because they
open the doors in the one case to the history

of a great people and in the other to one of
the noblest literatures and much of the best
thought mankind has yet produced. They
should be learned, because they enlarge the
mind and train and develop its powers. The
classics cannot longer hope to live on the theory that they are the sum of education, because this is false, and the falsehood kills.
But they will live forever on their own merits
as the voices of a great past in literature and
history which every well-educated man must
be able to hear and understand.

What matters it, so far as the glory of the
literature and the poetry is concerned, whether the men of whom Homer sang were leaders
of savage tribes or not? It matters nothing.
But it is of consequence that we should put
into Homer people who do not belong there,
and then give them out of our own ideas qualities they never had. Again the falsehood kills.
We love Homer, not because he drew a number of persons whom we have chosen to speak
of as heroes after the types of chivalry, ancient and modern, but because he has pictured to us in immortal verse part of the moving pageant of human life. He has stirred
and delighted generations of men by the creations of a genius and an imagination beside

which the modern literature which calls him
" primitive " looks as frail and small as the
Arab tent lurking in the shadow of the Pyra-
mids when we compare it with the mighty
mass of the royal sepulchres towering above
it. We love Homer for the beauty of his
poetry, for his descriptions of sea and land,
of morning and evening, of battles and sieges,
of men and women in their strength and love-
liness. Why should we seek to thrust into all
this imperishable beauty a set of persons who
have no business there, because they are the
creatures of our own brains, made after our own
fashions? It adds nothing to Homer to con-
fuse his poetry with the characters it portrays.
Of all people we should take Homer and
Homer's men exactly as they are, for of Homer
we can rightly use the words of the one great
genius who has soared far beyond him, and
say, as Shakespeare does:

"He is as true as truth's simplicity,
And simpler than the infancy of truth."

THE LAST PLANTAGENET

THE LAST PLANTAGENET

SOME one has said that "the youth of England take their theology from Milton and their history from Shakespeare." Whether the first proposition is true or false, there can be no doubt that the second holds good, not only as to the youth of England, but as to all who speak or read the English tongue. The history of England which Shakespeare wrote is the history we really know, and the kings he put upon the stage are those who are real and vivid to English-speaking people to-day. Whatever these sovereigns may have been in reality, we think of them now as Shakespeare drew them. His conception has become that of the English-speaking world, and will so remain.

Life-like as all these royal portraits are, however, there is one that stands out with peculiar vividness. This is the last Plantagenet, Richard III. Some of the historical plays are never acted, and others seldom and irregularly. But Richard III. is always upon the stage. The tragedy which bears his name goes far beyond the circle of those who read, and passes easily out of the range of occasional "runs" and scattered performances, which are the lot of its companions. It is intensely popular as a play. It packs theatres, it thrills audiences, it stirs the ambition of every aspiring tragedian, and it is ever before the public. Shakespeare's Richard is the best known ruler England has ever had, for he is as familiar to the shoeblack and the newsboy, innocent of all learning and shouting applause from the gallery, as he is to the patient scholar in his closet, giving laborious days and nights to the mending of a corrupt line, or the settlement of a doubtful reading for some vast *Variorum* edition of the great dramatist.

It is not a hold upon posterity, however, which any one need envy. Lord Lyndhurst said that the knowledge that Lord Campbell would write his biography added a new terror to death. If Richard could have known that his story would have been told solely by his enemies, and would then have passed into the hands of the mightiest genius among men, to be depicted with all the resources of consummate art and all the prejudices of a servant of

the Tudors, he might well have felt that there
was a new pang added even to the terrors of
a mediæval death - bed. Yet such has been
his fate. Shakespeare took the statements of
one of the King's bitterest enemies, and from
them developed the Richard that we know.
In the light of recent discoveries, it is possible now, in some measure, to see how near
the great poet came to the historic truth.
Richard is so distinct to us in the work of the
dramatist that his career is always interesting,
and has found many writers who have devoted to it much time and study. With the new
materials, however, which modern research
has discovered, the subject has risen from the
level of a merely curious inquiry about an interesting character and the events of a dark
period, to a plane where the great forces of
English history are disclosed, and something
more than a mere bloody struggle for personal
power is revealed.

The first step is to define the Richard we
know; the second is to compare this Richard
and the supposed events of his life with the
facts which the centuries have spared, and
which now, after long hiding, have been
brought to light. But few words are needed
to set forth Shakespeare's Richard, so well is

3

he known to us all. He appears in three plays — in the second and third parts of *Henry VI.*, as well as in the one that bears his own name, and is depicted with that force of drawing and warmth of color of which only one man in all literature is capable. · He is drawn with the utmost care and precision of definition, and his career is worked out with unsparing logic. From his first utterance to his last, there is not a break or a slip to mar the artistic completeness of the whole. The man stands before us with all his tendencies, motives, and passions laid bare, and their consequences are carried out with the relentless force of a syllogism.

Richard makes his first appearance in the second part of *Henry VI.*, when York summons his sons to back him in his claim to the crown.

"*Queen Margaret.*—His sons, he says, will give their words for him.

" *York.*—Will you not, sons?

"*Edward.*—Ay, noble father, if our words will serve.

"*Richard.*—And if words will not, then our weapons shall."

This first sentence defines him at once as

the fighter and the man of action. Then he bandies words with Clifford, who cries:

"Hence, heap of wrath, foul, indigested lump,
As crooked in thy manners as thy shape."

Thus he is immediately stigmatized as physically hideous, and the first prejudice—that of the eye—is roused against him. The battle of St. Albans follows. Richard kills the Duke of Somerset, and, apostrophizing the body, exclaims:

"Sword, hold thy temper; heart be wrathful still:
Priests pray for enemies, but princes kill."

The last line marks sharply the man whose theory of life is to kill all who cross his purposes, while, as the play closes, his prowess in the battle is also especially emphasized.

In the third part of *Henry VI.* Richard figures largely. He is always the great soldier of the Yorkists—the foremost in fight, the most bloodthirsty, and the one who is ever eager for action and for blows. It is he who rallies the army at Towton when both Warwick and Edward give way. It is he who rescues Edward when Warwick imprisons him, and it is Richard who leads the van at Barnet and Tewkesbury.

In this play his character is developed, and in the great speech which begins:

"Ay, Edward will use women honorably,"

his qualities and purposes are minutely set forth.

The play ends with the great scene in the Tower, which Cibber tacked on to his version of *Richard III.*, and which is therefore familiar to every one. Richard kills Henry, and, with a cynical jest upon his lips, goes his way.

In the tragedy which bears his name there is no need to trace him, for every one knows it well. It is easy to sum up his character, although an infinity of touches have gone to make the finished picture. In his full and final development Shakespeare's Richard is a complete monster, physically and mentally, without a redeeming moral trait, except a courage that knows no fear. He is a great soldier, a man of the highest ability—cold, determined, relentless. He is subtle, hypocritical, ingenious, with an iron will and an address which bends all things to his purpose. He is devoured by an ambition for the crown. In this he is the man of one idea, and never for a moment loses sight of his object. He has a savage wit, a biting sarcasm, a brutal frank-

ness, and, at the same time, a smooth, per-
suasive tongue in time of need. His most
marked trait, perhaps, is the cynicism with
which he meets every event, and which does
not spare even himself or his ambition. There
is no softer side, there are no periods of re-
morse. Moments of superstitious fear occur,
but these have no flavor of repentance, and as
soon as he can catch his breath these shadowy
terrors are trampled under foot. The qualities which are especially emphasized in Shakespeare's Richard are savage cruelty, indifference to bloodshed, ability, and a reckless fighting spirit, which finally brings him to his death.

Let us turn now to the facts of history, cold
and lifeless, with none of the glow of genius
upon them, and see how far the real Richard
was like the Richard of the poet. At the outset be it said that Shakespeare, with his marvellous insight into human nature, could not
be the mere reproducer of what Horace Walpole calls "mob stories and Lancastrian forgeries," however much he may have followed
them. With the sure intuition of genius he
saw much that he could not find in the books
he read, and all this came out in the picture.
For example, the ambition of Richard as

Shakespeare shows it was in the main true.
He came of a race who, for generations, had
been occupied in getting and holding thrones;
and his whole life had been absorbed, and all
his immediate family had been concerned, in
a struggle to seize and keep the crown. It is
no wonder that to him, so born and so bred,
the one thing worth having in life was the
royal crown of England.   In like manner
Shakespeare portrayed truly enough the
man's ability, his military capacity, his reckless personal courage, and his strong personal
influence over every one with whom he came
in contact.   These qualities, admitted alike
by friend and foe, we may take as undoubted.
All that remains is to see how far the other
features of Richard's character, as drawn by
Shakespeare, can be sustained by solid and
trustworthy historical evidence.

Shakespeare relied for his story upon the
account of Richard written by Sir Thomas
More, and the slightly varying versions of the
same narrative given by Hall and Holinshed.
Sir Thomas More's account is now known,
and is admitted by all recent authorities to
be, so far as the incidents go, the work of
Morton, Bishop of Ely, the one whom Richard sends in the play to get strawberries from

his garden in Holborn. Morton was one of
Richard's bitterest enemies, and a Lancastrian. Even if his narrative had been perfectly clear and consistent, the attitude of
the author to the subject would prevent its
being accepted on any point adverse to Richard without outside corroboration. But it is
not even consistent with itself, and can be
pulled to pieces by a critical examination almost without reference to other authorities.
Yet it was received for a long time as final,
and is still adhered to, even by modern
writers, to a surprising degree. The story
gained its authority chiefly from the fact that
it passed through the hands of Sir Thomas
More, who wrote it out in a dignified style,
and in language which was an immeasurable
improvement on any English prose that had
then appeared. It was this which gave it
weight and acceptance; and, as Dr. Mahaffy
says of Thucydides, it is astonishing how a
solemn manner and a noble style will carry
unsupported and unfounded statements without dispute for generations. The work was
left a fragment by its reputed author, and
was not published in his lifetime. It was not
an age of historical research. Sir Thomas
More made, and could have made, no inves-

tigation, in the modern sense. He simply took the tale as it was told him by his patron, dressed it in a fine style, and left it to posterity, who, receiving it through Shakespeare, has found it sufficient to damn Richard with for all time.

Rather more than a hundred years elapsed, and then Richard found a defender in Sir George Buck, an old antiquarian who died in 1623. After his death, what he had written about Richard was published, and he was set down as an untrustworthy lover of paradoxes, and passed unheeded. A century and a half went by, and then came another defender, in the person of Horace Walpole, with his *Historic Doubts*. The author's wit and reputation gained fame for the book, which showed much critical acumen, and which fatally discredited the received accounts. But it failed of its purpose, for it was regarded rather as the fanciful recreation of a literary epicure than as the serious historic criticism which it really was.

The present century has produced many painstaking and elaborate histories of Richard III. — notably Miss Halsted's and Sharon Turner's, both favorable to the King, and Jesse's on the other side. None of these writers, however, had access to the vast mass of state rolls and records which have lately been brought to light, and therefore they wrote at a disadvantage. Since then there have been two large works of authority on Richard — Mr. Gairdner's *Life*, and Mr. Legge's *Unpopular King*. Mr. Gairdner, a specialist on the period, an expert, and a trained historian, with the new material before him and completely master of it, has done more for Richard than any one else. He has adopted the adverse view, and has undertaken to sustain the traditional and Shakespearian account by the new evidence at his command. As he is perfectly candid, his failure to make the new and unimpeachable testimony bear out the old case is better for Richard's cause than any defence. For, if in his skilled hands the best testimony, beside which the traditional accounts have no standing, is unable to sustain the Shakespearian view, the break-down is fairly complete, and the time has arrived for the acceptance in history of a view of Richard and his reign very different from that popularly held.

Last of all comes Mr. Legge, as accurate and painstaking as Mr. Gairdner, with all the latter's material at his command, and some further new and important matter which he himself has discovered. Mr. Legge takes what may be called the modern and more favorable view, and supports his case strongly, although in his eagerness he falls into the very natural error of going too far, and of trying to show that Richard was right in all points and clear of blame in many cases where it is impossible to prove his innocence, and where, in the broad historical view, it is not very essential to the general theory to show anything of the kind.

Now let us consider the facts in Richard's case, not the various theories—for that would occupy volumes, and one hypothesis differs from another not in value, but in ingenuity. For the purpose of this brief study, the undisputed and reasonably certain facts are all we can deal with. Indeed, we have no right to go beyond the story they tell to reach a just conclusion.

Richard III. was the eleventh child and eighth son of Richard Plantagenet, Duke of York, and Cicely, daughter of the Earl of Westmoreland, of the great house of the Nevilles. His father was descended through the female line from Lionel, Duke of Clarence, third son of Edward III., and thus held an

unimpeachable hereditary title to the throne
as against the Lancastrians, who derived from
John of Gaunt, the fourth son of Edward III.

Richard was born at Fotheringay Castle, on
Monday, October 2, 1452. After his defeat
and death, it was stated that his mother was
pregnant with him for two years, that he was
brought into the world feet foremost by the
Cæsarean operation (an experience which his
mother, in a manner highly creditable to the
surgery of that period, seems to have survived
for more than thirty years), and that at his
birth he had a full set of teeth and long
hair down to his shoulders. These are unusual circumstances — all the more unusual
when we reflect that no one noted them at
the time, that there is not a scintilla of contemporary evidence to support them, that
they were never hinted at until forty years
after the event, and that they are absurd on
their face. Yet this silly fable has been made
part of the traditional Richard, most of it has
been gravely used by Shakespeare, and historians have seriously discussed it. It is, of
course, only fit, historically speaking, to be
consigned to the dust-heaps so much spoken
of by Carlyle.

Let us deal with the rest of the physical

horrors of Richard, and be rid of them all at once. His deformity is a great feature in Shakespeare, and is used with all Shakespeare's knowledge of human nature to explain much of what would be otherwise incredible. It is the bitterness of the deformed which makes Richard hate the world, which hardens his cruelty, and sharpens his already keen-edged ambition with the desire to overcome the scorn of mankind for defects he could not help, by reaching a place where he could put the world under his feet. Yet there is but little better evidence of his deformity than there is of his having been born with teeth.

The cheerful originator of both legends was one Rous, a monkish writer of Guy's Cliff. He wrote a eulogy of Richard while Richard reigned, and an invective against him after Henry VII. was on the throne. This fact alone disqualifies Rous as an authority, and it is not easy to understand why any one should take anything he wrote as by itself trustworthy testimony. Yet even Rous, with all his worthlessness, only said that Richard had the left shoulder a little lower than the right. The work of Morton and Sir Thomas More says the right shoulder was lower than the

left, and Polydore Vergil, who was not contemporary, says there was an inequality, but
does not mention which shoulder was the
higher. This conflicting evidence is all there
is on the subject, and it only proves that, if
there were any deformity, it was so trifling
that no one could tell exactly what or where
it was.

It is hardly necessary to call witnesses to
disprove such triviality as this, but it is easily
done, and the refutation is complete. No
contemporary other than Rous even alludes
to Richard's deformity, and these others who
are silent are the only writers of real authority. Fabyan, the Londoner, who must have
seen Richard often, and who was a Lancastrian, says nothing of any deformity. The
Croyland Chronicler, a member of Edward
IV.'s council, is equally silent, and so, too, is
Comines, although he twice speaks of Edward
as the handsomest prince he had seen, thus
showing that he noted physical appearance.
Stowe said he had talked with old men who
had seen Richard, and they declared "that
he was of bodily shape comely enough, only
of low stature." Even Rous himself, in his
portrait of Richard indicates no deformity.
The portraits indeed—and there are several

authentic examples—show us a man without any trace, either in expression or feature, of bodily malformation. The face is a striking one, strong, high-bred, intellectual, rather stern, perhaps, and a little hard in the lines, but not in the least cruel or malignant, and with a prevailing air of sadness.

The only other point to be considered in this connection occurs in the famous scene at the council board, where Richard, denouncing Hastings, bares his arm, shrunken and withered as it always had been, according to Morton, and says that it was due to the sorcery of the Queen and others. If it always had been withered, it is difficult to see how Richard could have been so dull as to suppose that, even in that superstitious age, he could make any one believe that his arm had been lately crippled by the machinations of the Queen and Jane Shore. The thing was in fact impossible. He very probably accused Hastings of witchcraft or conspiracy, or anything else, when he wished to sweep him from his path, but he bared no withered arm, because the King, who at Bosworth unhorsed Sir John Cheney, cut down Sir William Brandon, forced his way through ranks of fighting men nearly to Richmond himself, the general who led the van at Barnet and Tewkesbury, could not have been maimed in this way. The man who performed these feats of daring and of bodily strength must have been quick, muscular, and adroit, a vigorous rider, and skilled in the use of weapons. That he performed these precise feats is proved and unquestioned, and they were not performed by a man with a withered, shrunken, useless arm.

In the way of positive evidence we have the statement of the Countess of Desmond, quoted by Hutton, that Edward, who was notorious for his beauty, was the handsomest man present on a certain occasion, and that Richard was the next. So we may leave the deformity. There is a little poor evidence that it existed in a very trivial form. There is a great deal of good evidence that it did not exist at all. As a physical horror, an index to a black soul, which filled the on-looker with repulsion, the tradition of Richard's deformity is as idle a myth as that about his monstrous birth, and, like that, may be dismissed to the limbo of historical rubbish.

So far as the facts go, Richard was born much like other people, and did not differ from them in appearance by any malforma-

tion. We know nothing of his early child-
hood, except that he was with his mother in
England. During that time his father first
took up arms for the redress of abuses, then
asserted his claim to the crown, was constituted heir to the throne by Henry VI., and
finally was killed in the battle of Wakefield.
At this time Richard was eight years old, and
all the scenes of the play in which he appears
with his father as a full-grown fighting-man of
savage temper are necessarily pure invention.

After Wakefield, George and Richard were
sent by their mother for safety to the court
of Philip the Good, of Burgundy, whence they
returned to find their brother, victor in the
battles of St. Albans and Towton, firmly seat-
ed on the throne as Edward IV. George was
created Duke of Clarence, Richard Duke of
Gloucester and Admiral of the Sea, and large
estates were conferred on both. Richard
then appears to have been placed, for training
and education, under the guardianship of the
great Earl of Warwick. By the time he was
fifteen he was out of tutelage, and we hear of
him as chief mourner at the ceremonies incident to the reinterment of the bodies of the
Duke of York and the Earl of Rutland. A
little later we hear of him again with the

army upon the Scottish border, and we know that he was then leading an active military life.

Meantime Edward IV. made his foolish marriage with Elizabeth Woodville; the Woodville, or Queen's faction, rose to power, and a series of quarrels ensued with Warwick, which resulted in the great Earl going over to the Lancastrians. With him went the Duke of Clarence, moved thereto by hatred of the Woodvilles and by the temptation of becoming heir to the crown of Henry VI. The uprising which followed was completely successful. Edward was dethroned and deserted. He fled the kingdom to France, accompanied by Richard, who, boy as he was, remained faithful in the dark hour, while Clarence betrayed his brother, assisted in his overthrow, and plotted to get the throne himself.

Early in the next year, 1471, Edward and Richard landed in England with a mere handful of men, got possession of York, and thence marched rapidly on London, gathering strength as they advanced. Clarence now abandoned Warwick and came over to his brother's side —according to later authorities, induced to do so by the diplomacy of Richard. London re-

4

ceived Edward favorably, and on Easter eve
the brothers marched out and met Warwick
at Barnet. In the hard-fought battle of the
next day Richard, only nineteen years old, led
the van and bore the brunt of the fighting.
The Yorkists won, and Warwick was killed.
Meantime Queen Margaret and her son had
landed with a powerful army, and less than a
month later—on the 4th of May—Edward met
and defeated them at Tewkesbury. Again
Richard was given the most responsible post.
Again he led the van, and, storming the Duke
of Somerset's intrenched camp, won a quick
and decisive victory.

We have now come to the first of his stage
murders, in which Shakespeare represents him
as a leading participant, the killing of Prince
Edward, son of Henry VI. Mr. Gairdner,
though he does his best by it, honestly admits
that this affair is "a tradition of later times,"
which is a mild way of putting it. There is no
contemporary evidence to sustain the charge
that the King and his brothers stabbed young
Edward. The Croyland Chronicle, the Fleetwood Chronicle, Dr. Warkworth, and two manuscript contemporaries all say Edward was
slain " in the field." It is a distinct affirmative
statement. Fabyan later, and Lancastrian, says

the King, before whom Edward was brought,
struck the Prince with his gauntlet, and that
the boy was then slain by the "Kynge's servants." On this statement the fable was built,
and even this later writer makes no shadow
of accusation against the royal brothers, who
were certainly not the "Kynge's servants."
But the inferior and later evidence must give
way to the higher. The statement of the five
contemporaries, who agree with each other, of
whom one was present, and another a Lancastrian, by all rules of historical evidence must
be accepted as final. They say Edward was
slain in the field, and give no hint that he was
ever brought before the King at all. The
whole scene is an invention, but even if it were
not, there is not a suggestion, even in the later
writer, with whom the tale originated, that
Richard had anything to do with the killing
of the young Prince.

We now come to the second stage murder—
that of Henry VI.—which Richard in the play
commits single-handed. Henry VI. was confined in the Tower, and, after the battle of
Tewkesbury, the bastard Falconbridge, who
had command of the fleet, came to London
to liberate him and renew the struggle. Falconbridge was repulsed by the citizens and

retired to Kent, while Edward marched rapidly to London on hearing the news of the
revolt.   He arrived there May 21st, and passed
that night with his court in the Tower, where
were held a cabinet council and a great banquet.   The next day Richard set out for Can-
terbury in pursuit of Falconbridge.   On the
night of May 21st, while all these affairs of
business and pleasure were in progress, Henry VI. died, or was killed, in his neighbor-
ing prison.   The Fleetwood Chronicle, Yorkist,
says he died of "pure displeasure and melancholy" at the disaster which had befallen his
family.   As he was nearly, if not quite, imbecile, this story seems unlikely on its face.   The
Croyland Chronicle says that King Henry was
found lifeless, and that the "doer thereof deserves the name of tyrant," which, though
vague, can fairly point at only one person,
the King, Edward IV.   Dr. Warkworth says
that Henry was put to death, the "Duke of
Gloucester and many others being then at the
Tower."   Fabyan simply says the King "was
stykked with a dagger."   The later writers all
tell different stories, varying from Sir Thomas
More, who, of course, says that Richard killed
Henry with his own hand, to Habington, who
blackens Richard in every possible way, but

on this occasion defends him and charges the murder direct to Edward and his cabinet council.

That Henry was murdered there can be no reasonable doubt. The rising of Falconbridge had sealed his fate, and had shown that, imbecile though he was, he was still a source of danger. How he was killed no one but those directly concerned knew, and they did not tell. The manner of his death was unknown, but there is no evidence whatever of the first class to fix the actual killing on Richard and a good deal to fasten the responsibility on the King. Apart from the evidence, it is absurd to suppose that the King's brother should have played the part of an executioner. The Tower was swarming with the victorious Yorkists—soldiers of desperate character, inured to bloodshed — and the King's brother-in-law, Earl Rivers, was in command. Henry was a danger, and in the way, and it was not an age of scruples. But while generally for the interests of the House of York to be rid of him, it was the especial interest of Edward, and not of Richard, who was then too remote from the throne to be affected at all by Henry's existence. The natural explanation is the one best supported by such evidence as is worth con-

sidering, that Henry was put to death by Edward's order or with his sanction. That Richard approved the step it is reasonable to suppose. Most persons appear to have accepted
it as a painful but necessary political action,
for politics at that time were of that pleasant
cast. But that Richard was more responsible
than the rest of his family, there is no reason
to believe; and that he himself went sword in
hand and stabbed Henry is not sustained by
any good evidence, nor can it be accepted by
any fair rules of reasoning.

In any event, the House of York was now
firmly established, and the last Lancastrian of
the legitimate line was gone. For twelve years
Edward was to rule England undisturbed.
There is no need here to give any account
of his reign. It is enough simply to bring together the known facts about Richard during
that period. In the first hours of triumph he
received his share of the spoils, made larger by
the fidelity which he had shown when Clarence
played Edward false. He was appointed Lord
Chamberlain and steward of the Duchy of Lan-
caster, and received the forfeited estates of
Oxford, a portion of Warwick's, and the whole
of divers others. He also received the thanks
of Parliament, which indicates that he was

popular. Soon after this began the contest about his marriage with Anne Neville. The famous wooing scene in Shakespeare and his treatment of Richard's marital relations are pure invention. At the time of the Shakespearian wooing, which must have been May 22, 1471, Richard was in Kent quelling an insurrection, and Anne, who had not yet completed her fourteenth year, was a prisoner in the Tower, having been captured at Tewkesbury with Queen Margaret. She was never married to Prince Edward, and is spoken of as "puella" in the Croyland Chronicle. It is probable that she was betrothed to the Lancastrian Prince, although there are doubts even on this point.

The historic facts are that Richard and Anne were cousins, and had been brought up together, and that after the final settlement of Edward upon the throne Richard sought her in marriage. Anne, however, was the sister and co-heiress of Isabella, daughter of the great Earl of Warwick and wife of Clarence. The Duke of Clarence wished to get all the Warwick estates, and, having no mind to divide them with his brother, abducted Anne and hid her in London in the disguise of a kitchen-maid. Richard discovered her, took her away,

with her own apparent good-will, and put her
in sanctuary. Then came a fierce dispute between the brothers, who argued the case before
the council, and it was even feared that they
would take up arms. Finally the decision went
in Richard's favor. The King sustained him.
He got half of the Warwick estates, and married Anne, probably in 1473. There is no evidence to show that they lived together otherwise than happily, or that Richard ever neglected her. On the contrary, they were constantly together. She bore him children, one
of whom became Prince of Wales, and the in-
timation of Shakespeare that Richard had a
hand in her death is sustained by no evidence
worth considering.

˅ The four years succeeding the battle of
Tewkesbury, Richard, who was Warden of
the Marches and High Constable, spent almost entirely on the northern borders. It
was a difficult position, for there was much
disaffection in that region. Richard governed
wisely and well, and proved himself a strong
administrator. He achieved a popularity in
the north which never failed him, and even
after his death the people there defended his
memory.

In 1475 Edward, after burdening his sub-

jects with terrible taxation, raised a fine army
and invaded France. Once there, instead of
fighting and winning, as he undoubtedly
could have done, he came to a treaty with
Louis, and for money down and an assured
tribute, withdrew. All the great nobles and
courtiers about him were bribed largely and
openly, and gave their assent. Richard alone
stood out, refused all bribes, and denounced
the treaty as shameful. His attitude was as
well known as it was exceptional, and established his strength and popularity with the
people of England, who, wrung with taxation
for a war, resented bitterly the conclusion of
a sordid peace.

Soon after the King's return from France
the trouble with Clarence culminated. Edward had never been on good terms with his
brother George since the latter's double
treachery to himself and Warwick. He
treated him coldly, and discriminated against
him in exemptions and gifts. Clarence
sulked and withdrew from court. He was
rich and popular, he began to talk about the
bastardy of Edward's children, in which case
he was the next heir to the throne he had already tried to reach, and finally, on the death
of his wife, he set about to marry the daugh-

ter of Charles of Burgundy. In a word, he became dangerous. He was arrested, tried publicly, and condemned. The King gave the order for his death, urged thereto by the Woodville faction, but to save a public execution the Duke was assassinated in the Tower in 1478. There is not only no proof, or even hint of proof, that Richard had anything to do with it, but the only fact we know is that Richard endeavored to prevent extreme measures. Even Sir Thomas More admits that Richard's guilt was doubtful, and merely surmises that he really desired Clarence's death while he openly opposed it. Mr. Gairdner says that there is nothing in the original sources (which clearly prove Clarence's death to have been wholly of the King's doing) to connect Richard with the crime. Yet none the less, and this is a fair example of the way Richard has been treated, he endeavors to throw suspicion on him by showing that he received some advantages from Clarence's death in the way of an estate, and he hints that Richard's religious foundations at that period might have been works of repentance for his brother's execution. The plain truth, on all existing evidence, is that Richard had nothing to do with the death

of Clarence, except to try vainly to prevent it.

The year before Clarence's assassination
there were indications of difficulties with
Scotland, which were fomented by France,
and which culminated in war in 1481. Richard, as Lieutenant-General in the north, was in
command of the army. He took the town of
Berwick, marched on Edinburgh, and entered
the city, making a treaty or arrangement
with the Lords in control which satisfied the
English claims. He then marched back to
the borders, besieged and took the castle of
Berwick, and thus restored to England the
powerful fortress which Margaret and the
Lancastrians had surrendered to Scotland twen-
ty-one years before. Throughout he showed
the military ability and the administrative capacity for which he was always distinguished,
and he was thanked again for his services by
Parliament.

The following year, on April 9, 1483, Edward IV., worn out by dissipation, died of a
surfeit. Long years after, Tudor historians,
who felt it necessary to attribute all the cur-
rent mortality of that period to one source,
insinuated a suspicion that Richard, who had
not been in London for some time, and who

was then at his government in the north, was in some way responsible for the King's death. The story is so silly that it is not worth considering, and is abandoned even by those writers who take the traditional view of Richard. What concerns us here is to trace Richard's subsequent course.

Edward had endeavored to bring about some arrangement before his death which should prevent the war of factions and secure the peaceful accession of his son, Edward V., then in his thirteenth year. It was all in vain. The breath was hardly out of his body before the struggle was begun by the Woodville faction to get possession of the person of the young King and thereby of the government. The Marquis of Dorset, young Edward's half-brother, seized the treasury, and began illegally to equip a navy. The others undertook to raise an army to escort the King from Ludlow, and were only prevented from doing so, and compelled to cut the retinue down to two thousand men, by the efforts of Lord Hastings, one of the most powerful nobles in the country, and a bitter enemy of the Woodville faction. All these movements were distinctly treasonable, for Richard had been constituted by the will of Edward IV. guardian of his son and Protector of the realm. The contest, therefore, at the start, was between the lawful authority and a powerful faction headed by the Queen.

Richard, on his side, was as prompt as his adversaries. With a small following, and accompanied by the Duke of Buckingham, he started for London, and succeeded in intercepting the Prince's retinue at Northampton, the Prince himself having been hurried on to Stony Stratford. Briefly stated, Richard arrested Earl Rivers and Lord Grey, the King's uncle and half-brother, and Sir Thomas Vaughan, sent them to prison at Pontefract Castle, and then went on to Stony Stratford. Masters of the young King's person, Richard and Buckingham, then marched to London and established their charge in the Tower, which, it should be remembered, was at that period a palace quite as much as a prison. Meantime the Queen, the rising which she had projected having failed, had taken sanctuary with her daughter and her second son, the Duke of York, at Westminster. Then followed six weeks of plotting and intrigue. The Woodville faction held one council in the Tower, Richard another in Crosby Place. Lord Hastings, who had helped Richard against the

Woodvilles, had no mind to sustain him in power as Protector—still less as King—and Richard, acting with the suddenness and determination which were part of his character, arrested Hastings for high treason at a council meeting, and had him executed, without even a form of trial, that very afternoon. At the same time, Rivers, Vaughan, and Grey, after due trial, were executed at Pontefract.

With the death of Hastings, Richard had swept his last powerful opponent from his path and was master of the situation. From this point he moved rapidly to the throne, which we cannot doubt he had intended to seize from the moment he heard of his brother's death. Into the management by which it was brought about, it is not necessary to enter. He based his claim on the bastardy of Edward's children, owing to the latter's precontract with Lady Eleanor Butler. This, although worthless in point of mere justice and according to the ideas of the present day, was at that period a perfectly good technical ground, and Richard produced direct evidence amply sufficient for his purpose. His case was considered so strong that, after his death, Henry VII. ordered all the petitions of the city of London, asking Richard to be King, and setting forth the reasons for the bastardy of his nephews, to be destroyed. The accidental preservation of one or two of these petitions has alone enabled us to know on what grounds Richard made his claims. By these it is also proved that the later historians falsified them in saying that they set forth a precontract between Edward and his mistress, Elizabeth Lucy, as given by Shakespeare, which was idle on its face, and in suppressing the real precontract with Lady Eleanor Butler, which was witnessed by Stillington, Bishop of Bath. Richard was unscrupulous, but he was not fatuous, and he did not attempt to impose on the public so feeble a story of the bastardy as that set forth by Shakespeare.

The city of London petitioned him to assume the crown. After a feigned declination he consented. The council confirmed the action. Parliament, which had been summoned, and then, by a writ of supersedeas—issued probably by the Woodville faction — postponed, met, nevertheless, and confirmed Richard's title, which was later confirmed again by a Parliament formally brought together. If the bastardy of Edward's children is not admitted, Richard, according to the ideas of that day, was, like Henry IV. and Henry VII., a usurper. According to modern theories, he was a constitutionally chosen King, with the election of lords, commons, council, and city, as much so as any ruler who ever sat upon the throne.

He secured the throne with far less blood-shed than marked any of the changes of the crown from the accession of Henry VI. to that of Henry VIII. He executed three noblemen representing the Woodville faction at Ponte-fract, and one, Lord Hastings, in London. His action in regard to the Woodvilles was popular, and is so admitted by all historians, for that faction was hated as oppressive and lux-urious. Hastings's death was regretted, but was regarded as a political necessity. Richard's management of the city and of his own claim to the throne was perfectly open, and he be-came King by the assent of every branch of the government and of the popular voice. What-ever his purposes—and they were no doubt as ambitious and selfish as his methods were violent and unscrupulous—it could not have been otherwise, for Richard did not have the usual weapon of usurpers, an army. It was reported that his forces from the north were coming, twenty thousand strong, to his sup-port. These troops did not arrive until after

Richard had assumed the crown, been proclaimed and accepted King, and taken the royal oath. When they came, there were only four or five thousand, according to Fabyan, raw levies in rusty armor and unfit really for service. They remained until after the coronation, but played no part, and were not considered as of any importance by the Londoners.

Richard, therefore, reached the crown in eight weeks, with no army at his back, and but trifling opposition. He could have effected this on only one condition. The community wanted him. If they had not, he would have been helpless and defeated at the start. It was natural enough, if we look at it without traditional prejudice. Richard was recognized as the ablest man in the kingdom, both as general and administrator. He had opposed the French peace, conquered Scotland, and brought peace to the borders. He was a strong man, capable of rule. On the other side was a boy King whose accession meant a period of violence and disorder as factions struggled for control, and that worst of all tyrannies, the rule of contending nobles. Richard offered the best chance of law, order, and strong government, and that is the sole

5

reason that he was able to carry his adroit schemes to such quick success.

The coronation took place almost immediately, on July 6th, and was performed with great splendor. The new King signalized his accession by a general pardon, extending his clemency even to some of the most bitter enemies of himself and his house. He then set out on a progress through the kingdom. Everywhere he was received with acclamation, and many of the towns voluntarily offered him gifts of money to defray the expenses of his journey, which is the strongest proof of his popularity. Such offers were rare at that period, but Richard declined them all. Every sign that we can now discover points to the fact that he himself was very popular, and that among the masses of the people his accession to the throne was regarded as the best thing that could have happened.

While he was on this progress the report went out that his nephews, the princes, had died by foul means in the Tower. Thus we come to the deed which has formed the darkest stain on Richard's character, and which has done more to damn him with posterity than all else. Yet, curiously enough, we know less about it and have less evidence

concerning it than any other event in his career. The narrative of Sir Thomas More,
which has always been the accepted version,
carries in itself its own refutation. No outside evidence is needed. Careful criticism of
the story, as More or Morton tells it, shows it
to be full of contradictions and impossibili-
ties. It falls to pieces on examination. Let
us put together what we actually know. The
young King, Edward V., went to the Tower as
soon as he arrived in London, in the spring of
1483. Late in June, just before Richard became King, the Queen-mother gave up the
second boy, the Duke of York, and he likewise went to the Tower. Early in the following autumn it was rumored that the royal
children were dead. Two of the contemporary chroniclers are entirely silent on the subject. The third merely mentions the report
of their death. Nothing was known clearly
at that time beyond the fact that a rumor to
that effect was abroad. Richard preserved
absolute silence. He never denied the rumor. He never declared the princes dead as
a means of perfecting his title. After his
death he was attainted, and in the bill of at-
tainder no mention is made of the murder of
the princes. His bitterest enemies did not

then number that among his crimes. Not until seventeen years after Richard's death, not until Perkin Warbeck had attempted to personate the Duke of York, and it had become the direct interest of Henry VII. to prove the death of the princes, did anything like a definite account of their taking off appear. It was then said that Tyrrel and Dighton had confessed to smothering the two boys in the Tower.

Sir James Tyrrel, who had been Master of the Horse under Edward IV. and Richard, and subsequently trusted and advanced by Henry VII., was then in prison for complicity in aiding the Duke of Suffolk, for which he was subsequently executed. Dighton, also in prison, was released and rewarded by Henry VII., because "his statement pleased him." What they really confessed, if anything, is unknown, for all we have is what the King "gave out"; and what the King "gave out" we know only by hearsay and report. This sums up all the meagre evidence in regard to the death of the princes; for the bones dug up in the reign of Charles II., and honored by royal burial, are worthless as testimony. They might have been the bones of any one, even of an ape, whose skeleton, found in a turret, passed for a time as that of Edward V., and the place where they were found does not agree with the accepted story, or indeed any other.

All that we actually know, therefore, is that the princes went into the Tower in the summer of 1483, and though it was generally believed, by their mother among others, that one escaped, there is no proof that they were ever seen again alive outside the Tower walls. We also know that it was rumored in the autumn of 1483 that they had been murdered, and there knowledge stops. They may have been murdered by Richard's order, or have died, being delicate boys, of neglect and confinement. They may have survived Richard, and died, or been murdered, under Henry, whose interest in having them dead was greater than Richard's, for Henry could not, without destroying his wife's title, admit their bastardy. One conjecture, so far as proof and contemporary evidence go, is just as good and almost as well supported as another. We can only fall back on general reasoning. There is no proof that they survived Richard; the rumor of their death started in his time, and it was to his interest to have them out of the way, as movements were on foot among the nobles to assert Edward V.'s claim to the crown. The fairest inference is that they were put to death by Richard's order, and, in the darkness that covers the whole business, an inference is all we have. The murder of the princes is the blackest crime charged to Richard, and although direct proof of it seems impossible, he cannot be relieved from it unless new and positive evidence to the contrary is discovered.

At the time when this sinister rumor started, Richard was confronted with a much more practical danger. The Duke of Buckingham, whom Richard had declined to make too powerful, went into open rebellion, influenced largely by Morton, Bishop of Ely, who had been committed to the Duke's charge as a prisoner. This revolt was a signal for like movements by Lancastrians, the remnants of the Woodvilles, and the Earl of Richmond. It was a formidable situation for a King scarcely three months on the throne. Richard met it with his accustomed courage and capacity. He raised forces, moved with his usual quickness, and struck hard. The risings in the south were crushed, Richmond was repulsed from the coast, while by great floods in the west Buckingham's army was broken and dispersed, and he himself made a prisoner, and promptly and justly executed for high treason.

This display of power brought quiet and gave Richard opportunity to enter on the public work of his short reign. It is only possible here to give a summary of what he accomplished, but that is sufficient to show, not only his wisdom and ability, but that he had a strong, new policy, which ran consistently through every act. It was this policy, vigorously carried out, which makes good Richard's place as the harbinger of the new epoch, which vindicates his ability as a statesman, and which at the same time wrought his destruction.

In the first place, he had two Parliaments in his short reign. The Plantagenets as a race were not afraid of Parliament, and in their struggles for power they were fond of appealing to the Commons and seeking a parliamentary title. There was nothing of the huckstering spirit which the Tudors showed, and still less of the quarrelsome timidity and bad faith of the Stuarts in the relations of the Plantagenets to their Parliaments. They were quite ready to fight with or domineer over a Parliament, but they were equally ready to meet with it and seek its assistance. Richard was conspicuous for this, and he was equally marked in his regard for the courts. Almost his first act was to take his seat with the judges on the King's Bench, and he devoted himself to re-establishing and strengthening the administration of justice between man and man, and to the enforcement of the laws for the protection of life and property. He abolished Benevo-lences, the most oppressive form of wringing money from individuals in the form of gifts. It was a cruel system, harsh, unequal, and in-determinate in the amounts demanded. For it he substituted, or rather relied on, taxation, which, if burdensome, was at least determinate in amount, and was imposed with some regard to equality and justice.

He prohibited the wearing of any badges or cognizances but those of the King. This was a fatal blow to the private armies of the great nobles, and meant the end of private wars and a check upon constant insurrection. It carried in principle the overthrow of the feudal system and the substitution of one responsible king for a multitude of irresponsible and petty ty-rants.

He gave his protection and patronage to the new learning. He was the friend of Caxton

and the encourager of printing, and ordered
that no obstacle should be placed in the way
of the introduction of books, and of all that
could promote the new art in the kingdom.
He devised a method of carrying despatches
and news, in which may be traced the first
germ of the letter post. He gave liberally to
the Church, after the fashion of his time; but,
superstitious as he was, he curbed the over-
grown power of the clergy, and sought to check
some of the gross abuses of the day by bringing them within the jurisdiction of the secular
courts. All this, in addition to extensive relations with foreign powers and several progresses
through the kingdom, represents a great work
for two troubled years, work that only a vigorous mind, filled with new and definite ideas,
could have conceived.

At the close of two years the end came.
Richmond landed with a mercenary force, and,
gathering some of the ever-ready and discon-
tented nobles, marched towards London. Richard rapidly raised a much more powerful army
and hastened to oppose him. They met at
Bosworth. The royal forces were made up on
the old feudal system of bands led by nobles,
and these bands looked for command to
their immediate chiefs and not to the King.

If the leaders failed or were false their troops
went with them, and this was precisely what
happened at Bosworth. There was really
hardly any battle at all, as we can see from
the trivial loss of the invaders. The Stanleys,
commanding two large bodies of troops, deserted the King's standard almost immediately, and then turned upon the army they
had betrayed. The royal forces were thrown,
of course, into panic and confusion. Richard
was urged to leave the field. He had ample
time and opportunity to escape, but he refused.
" I will die as I have lived," he said, " King
of England." The wild fighting spirit of the
Plantagenets was roused. Putting himself at
the head of a handful of faithful followers, he
charged straight into the enemy's lines, making
for Richmond himself. He unhorsed Sir John
Cheney, a knight of gigantic stature. He cut
down Sir William Brandon, Richmond's stand-
ard-bearer, and mortally wounded him. His
desperate valor brought him nearly to his rival,
and then the men of Stanley closed in around
him and he was beaten to the earth and killed
with a hundred blows from the hands of the
common soldiers. His crown was found later
in a hawthorn bush. His body disappeared.
There are various accounts as to what befel

it, but it is only certain that it was obscurely buried.

So fell the last Plantagenet, fittingly, upon the field of battle, heading a desperate charge. So fell also the first King who saw the coming of a new time in England, and who was great statesman enough to begin a policy which would break the power of the nobles, overthrow the feudal system, and bring from the union of crown and people law and order out of chaos and anarchy. The accepted tradition is that Richard was overthrown because he was so universally hated for his cruelty and tyranny that every one was eager to desert him and to compass his downfall at the first opportunity. For this tradition there is no solid foundation. To begin with, Richard was not a tyrant. All his legislation and his whole general policy were popular and liberal. As to his cruelty, admitting once for all every crime that can be charged against him on any reasonable evidence, the cold-blooded execution of Hastings, Rivers, Vaughan, and Grey, and the murder of the princes, there is no doubt that, according to the views of the nineteenth century, Richard was indifferent to human life, blood-thirsty, and cruel. He did not live, however, in the nineteenth but in

the fifteenth century. He lived among feudal
nobles, in a period of constant and savage war,
and in a society whose views as to the sacred-
ness of human life and as to murder, treachery,
and the like, were those of North American
Indians. If Richard be tried by the only
proper standard, that of his own time, he will
be found to be not more, but less, cruel and
bloody than either his predecessors or those
who came after him. The act which has
especially blackened his memory is the mysterious removal or murder of the princes.
Yet Clifford, backed by Margaret of Anjou,
had killed in cold blood Richard's brother,
the Earl of Rutland, a boy of sixteen, while
Henry VII. imprisoned and executed the
feeble-minded Earl of Warwick, the son of
Clarence. In mere numbers of executions,
excluding, of course, on both sides, those who
were taken in open rebellion, Richard has
much less to answer for than Queen Margaret or Henry VII., and far less than Henry
VIII., who put to death anybody who happened to be distasteful to him on political,
personal, or religious grounds. There was no
public opinion in that day against putting to
death any one who had played and lost in the
great struggle of politics. Executions were a

recognized part of the business. When the game went against a statesman in those days, as Mr. Speaker Reed once said, he did not cross the aisle and take his place as the leader of his Majesty's opposition; he was sent to the Tower and had his head cut off. *Autres temps, autres mœurs.* At every turn of the wheel in the long struggle between the Lancastrians and the Yorkists, the victorious party always executed every leader of the other side upon whom they could lay hands. Such were the rules of the society, and such the politics in which Richard was brought up, and he played according to those rules, without excess, paying the final forfeit himself with undaunted courage.

Nothing is further from the truth than the notion that Richard was unpopular with the masses of the people. He had never injured them, and they did not care how many nobles or princes he put to death. There is no evidence that there was any popular uprising against Richard at any time, but, on the contrary, all the evidence we have shows that he was supported and liked by the people, especially in the North, where he was best known. This was but natural. Richard represented law, order, and authority. All his legislation

was for the benefit of the people, and they
knew it. Their enemies and his were the
same, and they knew that too.

Yet it is true that Richard was hated. Fabyan records that there were mutterings against
him on the very day of his coronation, but the
men who muttered thus under their breath,
according to the old chronicler, were the nobles, not the people. Now we come to the
real unpopularity of Richard. He was hated
by the classes, not by the masses. The nobles
who had opposed him hated him because he
had beaten them; those who had supported
him, because they found a master where they
intended to have a puppet. All classes of
the nobility soon grew to hate him with a
common and bitter hatred, because they recognized in him the enemy of their order and
saw that every move he made tended to destroy their power. He was fighting the battle
of crown and people against the feudal system
of petty tyrants, and the nobles, who saw political and military ruin advancing upon them,
rose against the King who led the march.
They raised a rebellion under Buckingham
and failed. They took breath, set up a claimant to the throne, supplied him with forces,
and then, by treachery, wrecked the royal

army at Bosworth and slew their foe. It was their last effort; they were exhausted, and, although they had changed kings, they had not changed royalty or checked the movement of the time. The feudal system fell at Bosworth with the King who had given it its death-blow and marked out the road for his successor to follow.

It is here we come on the real importance of Richard III., when we find him a part of the great movement of the time, and leading the real forces which make history. If Richard's character as a man were all, it would not be more than a matter of curiosity to inquire into the truth concerning him. But behind this personal question there rises one of real importance, which has just been indicated, and to which those who have written upon him have given but little attention. On this side we are no longer dealing with doubtful or prejudiced chroniclers, no longer delving in dark corners whence the best issue is a probability. Here we come out into the broad light of day, where our authorities are the unquestioned witnesses of laws and state records, which tell us nothing of persons but much of things. In them, as we have seen, a strong, consistent policy is disclosed, and that policy reveals to us the great social and political change then in progress.

It was the period when an old order of life was dying and a new one was being born. The great feudal system of England was drawing to its unlamented close. It had worked out its destiny. It had rendered due service in its time, and had curbed the crown in the interests of liberty, but its inherent vices had grown predominant, and in this way it had come to be a block to the movement of men towards better things. In its development the feudal system had ceased to be of value as an aid to freedom against a centralized tyranny, and had become instead purely a dissolving and separatist force. When it culminated under Henry VI., we can see its perfect work. The crown, the central cohesive national power, had ceased to be. The real rulers of England were the great nobles, who set up and pulled down kings and tore the country with ambitious factions. Warwick was the arch-type, and the name he has kept through the centuries of the "King-maker" really tells the story. More men wore his livery and cognizance, more men would gather to the Bear and Ragged Staff of the Nevilles, than the King himself could summon. In a less degree all the great nobles were the same. Each was practically the head of a standing army. If the King did not please them, they took up arms, set up another King, and went to war. As they were always rent into bitter factions, the King could not please more than a portion of the nobility at any time, and the result was organized anarchy or the Wars of the Roses. The condition was little better than that which led Poland to ruin and partition.

The other powers in the state were King and people. To both the situation was hateful. The King did not like to hold his crown by sufferance and lie at the mercy of two or three powerful subjects. The people, especially in the towns, began to long for peace and order, and greatly preferred the chance of one man's tyranny to the infinitely worse oppression of a hundred petty tyrants. Steadily King and people were drawing together, and the only question was when they would be able to crush the feudal nobility and break their power. Edward IV. saw what it was necessary to do, and made some spasmodic efforts in the right direction. But Edward, although a brilliant general, was no statesman. He was too sensual, too indolent, too

6

worthless, except on the field of battle, for such work. Richard was as brilliant a soldier as Edward, but he was also a statesman, and he was neither sensual nor indolent. Short as his reign was, a great work was done, and we have seen that a clear, strong policy of maintaining law and order and of crushing the nobility runs in unbroken line through his statutes.

It was wise and able work. Unluckily for himself, although it made no difference in the result, Richard was just a little too early. The feudal nobility were dying, but not quite dead. There were still enough of them to set up a claimant for the crown, still enough to betray Richard and kill him on the field of battle. He was their enemy, and as a class they knew it. It was not his cruelty, even if we admit as true all the Shakespearian crimes. Executions and murders of royal and noble persons were too much the fashion of the day to base a campaign on for the crown. They called Richard tyrant and murderer and " bloody boar," and he retorted with proclamations in which he denounced them not merely as traitors but as murderers, adulterers, and extortioners. There was just as much truth in one charge as the other, and neither

was of any importance in the fight. Mr. Legge
is right in saying that there was no national or
popular uprising. Indeed, the people of York
mourned publicly over Richard's "treacherous
murder," when such lamentation was far from
safe, and quarrelled in defence of his memory
six years later. There was, in reality, no reason
for a popular revolt against Richard, for, as has
been shown, all his legislation and public acts
made for the benefit of the people as much as
of the crown, and, as Richard represented the
new movement in politics, they were bound to
do so.

If Richard had been a little more thorough
and a little more cruel, if he had sent Lord
Stanley to the block, as he was warranted in
doing by the code of the day, if he had sent
Stanley's wife along the same road, and procured, as he might have done, the murder of
the Earl of Richmond, all would have gone
well with him. He would have died, probably,
according to his sneer, "a good old man," and
he would have left an immense reputation as
the King who stamped out feudalism, opened
the door to learning and civilization, brought
crown and people together, consolidated the
English monarchy, and set England on the
triumphant march of modern days. His exe-

cutions and cruelties would have been glossed
over, and his exploits and abilities enlarged.
But he struck the first intelligent blow from
the throne at the anarchic nobility, and they
had still strength to return the blow, kill him,
and then load his memory with obloquy.

Richard's immediate vindication as a statesman lies in the fact that his successor continued
his policy, and, enforcing the law against private liveries, fined heavily his great supporter,
the Earl of Oxford, because, on a royal visit,
the Earl received him with two thousand retainers wearing the cognizance of the house of
Vere. The movement towards the consolida-
tion of the monarchy and the development of
the people as a force proceeded from the points
fixed by the last Plantagenet. Richard came
just at the dawn of the new movement, and
thus marks by his reign no less than by his
legislation a turning-point of momentous importance in the history of the English-speaking
race.

He was the beginner of new things, but he
was also the end of an old order. He was the
last of a great dynasty. For nearly four hundred years the Plantagenets held the English
throne. In all history there has never been of
one blood and of one lineage, unbroken and un-

tainted, a reigning family which has shown so
much ability of so high an order. They produced great soldiers and great statesmen, and
these were the rule. The weaklings were only a
few marked exceptions. They were, essentially,
a royal, ruling, fighting race, and their end was
coincident with that of the old feudal nobility
and its system. The change was startling. The
great dynasty of fighting monarchs and statesmen was succeeded by a set of bourgeois kings.
Henry VII. was the grandson of an obscure
Welsh gentleman, and his methods answered
to his origin. He was a shrewd, able man, unscrupulous and crafty, every whit as cruel as
Richard, and, as Horace Walpole says, one of
the "meanest tyrants" who ever sat upon a
throne. He recognized in the light of what
Richard had done the true forces of the time,
and went with them. But the old conquering, adventurous spirit of the Plantagenets had
gone and the bourgeois monarchy had come.
A bourgeois monarchy it remained, despite the
false romance cast over the Stuarts, and it became more so than ever when a third-rate
German family was called to the throne. In
the four hundred years since the Plantagenets
there have been three dynasties in England,
besides Oliver Cromwell and William of Orange.

Among them all, since the last Plantagenet fell at Bosworth, closing a long line of statesmen and warriors, England has had but two great rulers, and one was a country squire, the other, a Dutch prince. There was ability in the Tudors, and common-sense, much meanness and cruelty, and highly imperfect morals. Of the Stuarts, Charles II. had some sense, but the rest had neither sense nor morals, and were as worthless a family as accident ever brought to a crown. The Guelphs have answered their purpose, but it would be flattery to call them mediocre in ability. It is a picturesque contrast to the brilliant Plantagenets, and yet it must be admitted that these mediocre bourgeois sovereigns, in the main plain and sensible folk, have been best probably for England and for the marvellous development of her people.

The change in the nobles was no less sharp than in the occupants of the throne. The old feudal nobility was practically extinct when Henry VII. came to the throne, and new men took their places. This old nobility had grievous faults, and their political system was deadly. They were sunk in superstition; not merely the superstition of the Church, but that of the necromancer and the witch, the wizard and the soothsayer. In cruelty and bloodshed they had the habits of Red Indians. They were illiterate, tyrannical, vindictive, and often treacherous. Yet, despite all this, they were brave and adventurous, a fighting, conquering, ruling class. As to the crown a bourgeois monarch, so to the dead feudal nobility a bourgeois nobility succeeded. Empson and Dudley typify at the worst the new men who rose to power under Henry VII. The new nobility was a land-grabbing, money-getting set. They plundered the Church and seized her lands; they inclosed the commons and added them to their domains. As a class, they were sharp political managers, rarely statesmen, and they had none of the bold, adventurous spirit of their predecessors. They made no wars, they sought no conquests, they engaged in no dangerous enterprises. If the old nobility had the failings usually attributed to pirates, their successors had the faults commonly given to usurers.

Last remained the people, who were neither extinct nor dethroned, but who were just taking the first painful steps which were to lead them to supremacy. The abolition of military tenures and the break-down of the feudal system wrought a great change in their condition. Villanage disappeared, and from holding land by military service they became rent-payers. Then the commons were inclosed, and the struggle for life became desperate. Some were forced down until they sank into agricultural laborers. Others remained tenant farmers; others rose to be small squires and country gentry. Very many were forced off the land and took to the sea, to trade, to the professions. In the earlier days the daring English spirit was embodied in her Plantagenet kings and her feudal nobility. After the coming of the bourgeois monarchy that spirit deserted kings and nobles, but it was as strong and undimmed as ever in the descendants of the men who had drawn the bow and followed the Edwards and the Henrys at Poictiers and Cressy and Agincourt. While the bourgeois kings and nobles controlled England, she displayed, as a nation, none of the old spirit. We find it then only in men like Drake and Raleigh, but they came from the people, from the old fighting stock. At last crown and people clashed, and under Cromwell England rose once more to the rank of a great power, able to dictate to Europe. The Plantagenet spirit came again with the man of the people. There was a brief interregnum, then the de-

scendants of the feudal retainers consolidated
and obtained control of the nation; and, beginning with William and Marlborough, England entered on that wonderful course of conquest and extension which ran through the
whole eighteenth century, and subdued new
continents and old civilizations alike. The
spirit of the Plantagenets and their nobles
came to a new and more glorious being
among the descendants of the men who had
followed them, and while the bourgeois nobility produced the Duke of Newcastle, the
commons of England gave her the elder Pitt.

Such was the change which began under
Richard III., and which modern research among
rolls and records has brought to light by ex-
hibiting to us the course and purpose of his
legislation. The importance of his place in
history is plain enough to those who care to
look into it with "considerate eyes." The
ability of the man, his greatness as a soldier,
his wisdom as a statesman are also clear.
These things were his alone; while his crimes
and his overmastering ambition, although his
own too, were also the offspring of his times,
of which he, like other men, was the child and
prototype.

Yet the helplessness of history when it

comes in conflict with the work of a great imagination has never been more strikingly shown than in the case of the third Richard. Historians and critics may write volumes, they may lay bare all the facts, they may argue and dissect and weigh and discuss every jot and tittle of evidence, but, except to a very limited circle, it will be labor lost so far as the man Richard is concerned. The last Plantagenet will ever remain fixed in the popular fancy by the unsparing hand of genius. To the multitude who read books, to the vaster and uncounted multitude who go to the theatre, there will never be but one Richard—the Richard of Shakespeare. There, in the drama and on the stage, he has been fixed for all time, and nothing can efface the image. He will be forever, not only to the English-speaking world, but to the people of Europe, to whom Shakespeare's language is an unknown tongue, the crook-backed tyrant. Always, while art and letters survive, will the last Plantagenet limp across the stage, stab Henry with a bitter gibe, send Clarence to his death with a sneer, and order Buckingham and Hastings to execution as he would command his dinner to be served. The opinion of posterity probably does not trouble

Richard much since the event at Bosworth; but if it did, he nevertheless has one compensation for all the odium which has been heaped upon him. Despite the lurid light in which he appears, it is still he, and not his rival, who has the plaudits of the countless people who have watched, and will yet watch, his career upon the mimic stage. They know that he is a remorseless usurper, a devil incarnate, for it has been set before them with the master's unerring art. But the same art has shown them the man's ability and power, his force of will, and his dauntless courage. When the supreme moment comes, the popular sympathy is not with Henry, loudly proclaiming his virtuous sentiments, but with his fierce antagonist. The applause and cheers which greet the final scene are not for the respectable Richmond, but for him who kills five Richmonds, who enacts more wonders than a man, and who dies King of England, hemmed in by enemies, as full of valor as of royal blood, desperate in courage as in all else, fighting grimly to the last like a true Plantagenet.

SHAKESPEARE'S AMERICANISMS

SHAKESPEARE'S AMERICANISMS

MUCH has been written first and last about certain English words and phrases which are commonly called "Americanisms." That they are so classified is due to our brethren of England, who seem to think that in this way they not only relieve themselves of all responsibility for the existence of these offending parts of speech, but that they also in some mysterious manner make them things apart and put them outside the pale of the English language. No one would be hard-hearted enough to grudge to our island kindred any comfort they may take in this mental operation, but that any one should cherish such a belief shows a curious ignorance, not merely as to many of the words in question, but as to the history and present standing of the language itself. To describe an English word or phrase as American or British or Australian or Indian or South African may be convenient if we wish to define that portion of

the English-speaking people among whom it
originated or by whom it has been kept or
revived from the usage of an earlier day.
But it is worse than useless to do so if an
attempt to exclude the word from English
speech is thereby intended. It is no longer
possible in any such fashion as this to set
up arbitrary metes and bounds to the great
language which has spread over the world
with the march of the people who use it.
The "Queen's English" was a phrase correct
enough in the days of Elizabeth or Anne,
but it is an absurdity in those of Victoria.
In the time of the last Tudor or the last
Stuart every one whose native tongue was
English could be properly set down as a subject of the English Queen. No such proposition is possible now. The English-speaking
people who owe no allegiance to England's
Queen are to-day more numerous than those
who do.

In the face of facts like these it is just as impossible to set limits to the language or to establish a proprietorship in it in any given place
as it would be to fetter the growth of the people who speak it. It is the existence of these
conditions which also makes it out of the question to have any fixed standard of English in

the narrow sense not uncommon in other languages. It is quite possible to have Tuscan Italian or Castilian Spanish or Parisian French as the standard of correctness, but no one ever heard of " London English " used in that sense. The reason is simple. These nations have ceased to spread and colonize or to grow as nations. They are practically stationary. But English is the language of a conquering, colonizing race, which in the last three centuries has subdued and possessed ancient civilizations and virgin continents alike, and whose speech is now heard in the remotest corners of the earth.

It is not the least of the many glories of the English tongue that it has proved equal to the task which its possessors have imposed upon it. Like the race, it has shown itself capable of assimilating new elements without degeneration. It has met new conditions, adapted itself to them, and prevailed over them. It has proved itself flexible without weakness, and strong without rigidity. With all its vast spread, it still remains unchanged in essence and in all its great qualities.

For such a language with such a history no standard of a province or a city can be fixed in order to make a narrow rule from which no

7

appeal is possible. The usage of the best writers for the written, and of the best educated and most highly trained men for the spoken word, without regard to where they may have been born or to where they live, is the only possible standard for English speech. Such a test may not be very sharply defined, but it is the only one practicable for a language which has done so much, and which is constantly growing and advancing. As a rule of conduct in writing or speaking it is true that this kind of standard may be in unessential points a little vague. But this defect, if it be one, is outweighed a thousand times by the fact that the language is thus freed from the stiffness and narrowness which denote that the race has ceased to march, and that expansion for people and speech alike is at an end.

Yet the changes made during this world-wide extension, with all the infinite variety of new conditions which accompanied it, are, after all, more apparent than real. That they should be so few and at the same time so all-sufficient for every fresh need that has arisen demonstrates better than anything else the marvellous strength and richness inherent in the English language. In some cases new words have been invented or added to express new facts or new things, and these are both valuable and necessary. In other cases old words, both in the mother-country and else-where, have, in the processes of time and of altered conditions, been changed in meaning and usage, sometimes for the better and some-times for the worse. In still other instances old words and old meanings have lived on or been revived by one branch of the race when given up or modified elsewhere.

It is this last fact which makes it so futile to try to shut out from the language and its liter-ature certain words and phrases merely because they are not used in the island whence people and speech started on their career of conquest. It does not in the least follow, because a word is not used to-day in England, that it is either new or bad. It may be both, as is the case with many words which have never travelled beyond the mother-country, and with many others which have never been heard in the par-ent-land. On the other hand, it may equally well be neither. The mere fact that a word exists in one place and not in another, of itself proves nothing. That those of the English-speaking people who have remained in Great Britain should condemn as pestilent innovations words which they do not use themselves is very natural, but quite unscientific. It is the same attitude as that of the Tory reviewer who condemned some of James Russell Lowell's letters as " provincial." They are different in tone and thought from that to which he is accustomed, and hence he asserts that they must be bad. The real trouble is merely that the letters are American and not English, continental and not insular. They are not in the language or the spirit of the critic's own parish ; that is all. They jar on his habits of thought because they differ from his standard, and so he sets them down as provincial, failing hopelessly to see that mere difference proves nothing either way as to merits or defects. So a word used in the United States and not in England may be good or bad, but the mere fact that it is in use in one place and not in the other has no bearing as to either its goodness or the reverse. Its virtues or its defects must be determined on grounds more relative than this.

The best proof of the propositions just advanced can be found by examining some of the words which exist here and not in Great Britain, or which are used here with a meaning differing from that of British usage. It is well

to remember at the outset that the English
speech was planted in this country by English
emigrants, who settled Virginia and New England at the beginning of the seventeenth century. To Virginia came many educated men,
who became the planters, land-owners, and leaders of the infant State, and, although they did
little for nearly a century in behalf of general
education, the sons of the governing class were
either taught at home by English tutors or sent
across the water to English colleges. In New
England the average education among the first
settlers was high, and they showed their love
of learning by their immediate foundation of
a college and of a public-school system. The
Puritan leaders and their powerful clergy were,
as a rule, college-bred men, with all the traditions of Oxford and Cambridge fresh in their
minds and dear to their hearts. They would
have been the last men to corrupt or abuse the
mother-tongue, which they cherished more than
ever in the new and distant land. The language
which these people brought with them to Virginia and Massachusetts, moreover, was, as Mr.
Lowell has remarked, the language of Shakespeare, who lived and wrote and died just at the
period when these countrymen of his were taking their way to the New World. In view of

these latter-day criticisms, it might seem as if these emigrants ought to have brought some kind of English with them other than that of Shakespeare's England, but, luckily or unluckily, that was the only mode of speech they had. It followed very naturally that some of the words thus brought over the water, and then common to the English on both sides of the Atlantic, survived only in the New World, to which they were transplanted. This is not remarkable, but it is passing strange that words not only used in Shakespeare's time, but used by Shakespeare himself, should have lived to be disdainfully called " Americanisms " by people now living in Shakespeare's own country. It is well, therefore, to look at a few of these words occasionally, if only to refresh our memories. No single example, perhaps, is new, but when we bring several into a little group they make a picturesque illustration of the futility of undertaking to exclude a word from good society because it is used in one place where English-speaking people dwell and not in another.

What Mr. Bartlett in his dictionary of Americanisms calls justly one of "the most marked peculiarities of American speech " is the constant use of the word " well " as an in-

terjection, especially at the beginning of sentences.   Mr. Bartlett also says, " Englishmen
have told me that they could always detect
an American by this use of the word."   Here
perhaps is a clew to the true nationality of the
Danish soldiers with Italian names and idio-
matic English speech who appear in the first
scene of *Hamlet :*

> " *Bernardo.*—Have you had quiet guard ?
> " *Francisco.*—Not a mouse stirring.
> " *Bernardo.*—Well, good-night."

This is as excellent and precise an example
of the every-day American use of the word
" well " as could possibly be found.   The fact
is that the use of " well " as an interjection is
so common in Shakespeare that Mrs. Clarke
omits the word used in that capacity from her
concordance, and explains its omission on the
ground of its constant repetition, like " come,"
" look," " marry," and so on.   Thus has it
come to pass that an American betrays his
nationality to an Englishman because he uses
the word " well " interjectionally, as Shakespeare used it.   I have seen more than once
patronizing criticisms of this peculiarity of
American speech, but have never suffered at

the sight, because I have always been able to take to myself the consolation of Lord Byron, that it is

"Better to err with Pope than shine with Pye."

Our English brethren, again, use the word "ill" in speaking of a person "afflicted with disease"—to take Johnson's definition of the word "sick." They restrict the word "sick" to "nausea," and regard our employment of it, as applicable to any kind of disease, or to a person out of health from any cause, as an "Americanism." And yet this "Americanism" is Elizabethan and Shakespearian. For example, in *Midsummer-Night's Dream* (Act I., Scene I.), Helena says, "Sickness is catching," which is not the chief characteristic of the ailment to which modern English usage confines the word. In *Cymbeline*, again (Act V., Scene IV.), we find the phrase, "one that's sick o' the gout." Examples might be multiplied, for Shakespeare rarely uses the word "ill," but constantly the word "sick" in the general sense. In the Bible the use of "sick" is, I believe, unbroken. The marriage service says, "in sickness and in health," and Johnson's definition, as Mr. Bartlett points out, conforms to the usage of Chaucer, Milton, Dryden, and Cowper. Even the Englishman who starts with surprise at our general application of "sick" and "sickness," and who is nothing if not logical, would not think of describing an officer of the army as absent on "ill-leave" or as placed upon the "ill-list." The English restriction of the use of these two words is, in truth, wholly unwarranted, and should be given up in favor of the better and older American usage, which is that of all the highest standards of English literature.

The conditions of travelling have changed so much during this century, and all the methods of travel are so new, that most of the words connected with it are of necessity new also, either in form or application. In some cases the same phrases have sprung up in both England and the United States to meet the new requirements. In others, different words have been chosen by the two nations to express the same thing, and, so far as merit goes, there is little to choose between them. But there are a few words in this department which are as old as travelling itself, and which were as necessary in the days of the galley and the pack-horse as they are in those of the steamship

and the railroad. One of them is the com-
prehensive term for the things which travellers
carry with them. Englishmen commonly use
the word "luggage"; we Americans the word
"baggage." In this habit we agree with Touchstone, who, using a phrase which has become
part of our daily speech, says (Act III., Scene
II.), " though not with bag and baggage, yet
with scrip and scrippage." Leontes also, in the
Winter's Tale (Act I., Scene II.), employs the
same phrase as Touchstone. It may be argued that both allusions are drawn from military language, in which "baggage" is always
used. But this will not avail, for "luggage"
occurs twice at least in Shakespeare, referring
solely to the effects of an army. In *Henry V.*
(Act V., Scene IV.) we find "the luggage of
our camp"; and Fluellen says, in the same
play (Act IV., Scene VII.), "Kill the poys
and the luggage!" Shakespeare used both
words indifferently in the same sense, and the
" Americanism " was as familiar to him as the
" Briticism."

In this same connection it may be added
that the word "trunk," which we use where
the English say "box," is, like "baggage,"
Shakespearian. It occurs in *Lear* (Act II.,
Scene II.), where Kent calls Oswald a "one-

trunk-inheriting slave." Johnson interpreted this to mean "trunk-hose," which makes no sense. Steevens said "trunk" in this connection meant "coffer," and that all his property was in one "coffer" or "trunk." This seems to have been the accepted version ever since, as it is certainly the obvious and sensible one.

Almost always the preservation or revival of a Shakespearian word is something deserving profound gratitude, but the great master of English gives some authority for one distasteful phrase. This is the use of the word "stage" as a verb in the sense of to put upon the stage, a habit which has become of late sadly common. So the Duke, in the first scene of *Measure for Measure*, says :

"I love the people,
But do not like to stage me to their eyes."

Again, in *Antony and Cleopatra* (Act III., Scene XI.), "be stag'd to the show, against a sworder." And again, later in the same play (Act V., Scene II.), Cleopatra says :

"the quick comedians
Extemp'rally will stage us."

It is true that these examples all refer to persons and not to "staging plays," as the phrase runs to-day, but the use of the word, especially in the last case, seems identically the same.

Among characteristic American words none is more so than "to guess," in the sense of "to think." The word is old and good, but the significance that we give it is charged against us as an innovation of our own, and wholly without warrant. One sees it continually in English comic papers, and in books also, put into the mouths of Americans as a discreditable but unmistakable badge of nationality. Shakespeare uses the word constantly, generally in the narrower sense where it implies conjecture. Yet he also uses it in the broader American sense of thinking. For example, in *Measure for Measure* (Act IV., Scene IV.), Angelo says, "And why meet him at the gates, and redeliver our authorities there?" To which Escalus replies, in a most emphatically American fashion, "I guess not." There is no questioning, no conjecture here. It is simply our common American form of "I think not." Again, in the *Winter's Tale* (Act IV., Scene III.), Camillo says, "Which, I do guess, you do not purpose to him." This is the same use of the word in the sense of to think, and other instances might be added.   In view of this it seems not a little curious that a bit of Shakespeare's English, in the use of an excellent Saxon word, should be selected above all others by Englishmen of the nineteenth century to brand an American, not merely with his nationality, but with the misuse of his mother-tongue.   Be it said also in passing that "guess" is a far better word than "fancy," which the British are fond of putting to a similar service.

Leaving now legitimate words, and turning to the children of the street and the market-place, we find some curious examples, not only of American slang, but of slang which is regarded as extremely fresh and modern. Mr. Brander Matthews, in his most interesting article on that subject, has already pointed out that a "deck of cards" is Shakespearian.   In *Henry VI.* (Third Part, Act V., Scene I.), Gloucester says:

' But while he thought to steal the single ten,
  The king was slyly fingered from the deck."

Mr. Matthews has also cited a still more remarkable example of recent slang from the Sonnets—of all places in the world!—where "fire out" is apparently used in the exact colloquial sense of to-day. It occurs in the 144th Sonnet:

> "Yet this shall I ne'er know, but live in doubt
> Till my bad angel fire my good one out."

"Square," in the sense of fair or honest, and the verb "to be square," in the sense of to be fair or honest, are thought modern, and are now so constantly used that they have well-nigh passed beyond the boundaries of slang. If they do so, it is but a return to their old place, for Shakespeare has this use of the word, and in serious passages. In *Timon of Athens* (Act V., Scene V.), the First Senator says:

> "All have not offended ;
> For those that were, it is not square to take
> On those that are, revenges."

In *Antony and Cleopatra* (Act II., Scene II.) Mecænas says, "She's a most triumphant lady, if report be square to her."

Very recent is the use of the word "stuffed," particularly in American politics, to denote contemptuously what may be most nearly described as large and ineffective pretentiousness. But in *Much Ado about Noth-*

ing (Act I., Scene I.) the Messenger says, " A lord to a lord, a man to a man ; stuffed with all honorable virtues." To which Beatrice replies, " It is so, indeed ; he is no less than a *stuffed man :* but for the stuffing,—Well, we are all mortal." Here Beatrice uses the phrase " stuffed man " in contempt, catching up the word of the messenger.

"Flapjack," perhaps, is hardly to be called slang, but it is certainly an American phrase for a griddle-cake. We must have brought it with us, however, from Shakespeare's England, for there it is in *Pericles* (Act II., Scene I.), where the Grecian—very Grecian—fisherman says, " Come, thou shalt go home, and we'll have flesh for holidays, fish for fasting days, and moreo'er puddings and flapjacks; and thou shalt be welcome."

"Mad," in the sense of angry, is usually regarded in England as peculiarly American and a very improper use of the word. In *Romeo and Juliet* (Act III., Scene V.), Lady Capulet says to her husband, " You are too hot," and he replies, " God's bread ! it makes me mad," which, taken in connection with Lady Capulet's phrase, seems to bring the word " mad " clearly within the American usage. But however this may be, it is certain

that in Pepys's time "mad" in the sense of
angry was a common colloquial usage (*c.g.*,
Pepys, II., 72). This, therefore, is again one
of the Americanisms we brought with us from
England.

I will close this little collection of Shakespeare's Americanisms with a word that is
not slang, but the use of which in this country
shows the tenacity with which our people have
held to the Elizabethan phrases that their ancestors brought with them. In *As You Like
It* (Act I., Scene I.), Charles the Wrestler
says, "They say many young gentlemen flock
to him every day, and fleet the time careless-
ly, as they did in the golden world." "Fleet,"
as a verb in this sense of "to pass" or "to
move," may yet survive in some parts of England, but it has certainly disappeared from
the literature and the ordinary speech of both
England and the United States, except as a
nautical phrase. It is still in use, however, in
this exact Shakespearian sense in the daily
speech of people on the island of Nantucket,
in the State of Massachusetts. I have heard
it there frequently, and it is owing no doubt
to the isolation of the inhabitants that it still
lingers, as it does, an echo of the Elizabethan
days, among American fishermen and farmers

in the closing years of the nineteenth century.

In tracing a few Americanisms, as they are called, to the land whence they emigrated so many years ago, I have not gone beyond the greatest master of. the language. A little wider range, with excursions into other fields, would furnish us with pedigrees almost as good, if not quite so lofty, for many other words and phrases which are set down by the British guardians of our language as "Americanisms," generally with some adjective of an uncomplimentary character. But such further collection would be merely cumulative. These few examples from Shakespeare are quite sufficient to show that because a word is used by one branch of the English-speaking people and not by another, it does not therefore follow that the word in question is not both good and ancient. They prove also that words which some persons frown upon and condemn, merely because their own parish does not use them, may have served well the greatest men who ever wrote or spoke the language, and that they have a place and a title which the criticisms upon them can never hope to claim.

There is here a little lesson which is well

8

worth remembering, for the English speech is
too great an inheritance to be trifled with or
wrangled over.   It is much better for all who
speak it to give their best strength to defend-
ing it and keeping it pure and vigorous, so
that it may go on spreading and conquering,
as in the centuries which have already closed.
The true doctrine, which may well be taken
home to our hearts on both sides of the water,
has never been better put than in Lord Hough-
ton's fine lines:

> "Beyond the vague Atlantic deep,
>   Far as the farthest prairies sweep,
>   Where forest glooms the nerve appal,
>   Where burns the radiant Western fall,
>   One duty lies on old and young—
>   With filial piety to guard,·
>   As on its greenest native sward,
>   The glory of the English tongue.
>
> "That ample speech! That subtle speech!
>   Apt for the need of all and each:
>   Strong to endure, yet prompt to bend
>   Wherever human feelings tend.
>   Preserve its force; expand its powers;
>   And through the maze of civic life,
>   In Letters, Commerce, even in Strife,
>   Forget not it is yours and ours."

CHATTERTON

CHATTERTON

WE have the high authority of Major Pen-
dennis for the statement that this is a very un-
charitable world, and there can be no doubt
that, in practice, success succeeds, while failure
goes out into the cold air of neglect and for-
getfulness. Yet as human nature is not only
complicated, but contradictory, humanity has
a great deal of sentimental pity for itself, which
it is fond of showing in various ways. How
commonly, for example, do we hear it said of
families in which one member has attained distinction and success that some other member
was really the most brilliant, although he has
never come to anything at all, perhaps has come
to even worse than nothing. There is probably
no truth whatever in statements of this kind,
but it is often soothing, nevertheless, to believe
them. It is the same with those who die very
young. Not only have we declared as a maxim
that those who thus die are beloved of the
gods, but we are prone to believe and assert

that they are or would have been the superiors
in beauty, character, and intellect of those who
have the misfortune to tamely survive and live
out more or less effectively the allotted span
of life.   This is, after all, a gentle, kindly sentiment, at which we may smile, but with which
only the sourest of misanthropes would quarrel;
and it matters little whether it has or has not
the further merit of exact truth.   But when one
of those who have died ere their prime has
really given signs of exceptional promise, when
it has been possible to believe that a dawning
genius has been swept away by envious fate,
then imagination comes to the aid of pity, and
we readily make a marvel of him whose life has
been untimely cropped, for what might have
been is not tied down by the hard facts which
fetter what is.

To early deaths we owe three of the noblest
poems in the language — "Lycidas," "Ado-
nais," and "In Memoriam." Of the subject
of "Lycidas" we know only that he was a
young scholar named King, and that Milton
immortalized his memory; and of Arthur
Hallam but little more than that he was a
youth of rare promise and a friend of Tennyson. Keats, young as he was, left enough
of accomplished work to take him out of the

range of speculation and place him securely
in the first rank of great English poets. But
there are others in our literature beloved of
the gods who did not have Milton or Shelley
or Tennyson to mourn for them in imperishable verse, who yet have appealed strongly to
human sympathy and imagination, and whose
names, at least, are familiar and high-placed.
Among them the most conspicuous undoubtedly is Chatterton. His name, indeed, is better known than that of many men who have
filled large places in our literature; and there
is a general conviction that he was a genius,
although it is doubtful if any one except his
editor or biographer could be found who could
quote a line of his works. Chatterton's fame
has come primarily from the events of his own
brief life, and the world has been content to
take his genius on trust. This is natural enough,
for that life-story was one to appeal most strongly to both our feelings and our imagination.
He was a mere boy, and yet he had perplexed,
if not deceived, the literary and critical world
of his day by a series of forged poems. He
was also a prolific writer apart from this. He
fought a desperate battle with adverse fate, and
died in misery, by his own hand, before he was
twenty. The dead boy on his miserable bed

in a squalid garret has been made familiar to
us by the painter, while the playwright and the
actor have put his struggle for life and glory
before us on the stage.   Every one knows the
name and the story, and has sighed over the
picture and the play.   Very few, probably,
know more, and perhaps it might be best to
end there, and not inquire further.   Fate dealt
hardly with Chatterton, and the fame he fought
for came only after his death.   He certainly
suffered enough to have it given to him freely,
even if it rests merely on the sad and romantic
story of his life.   Yet one hardly likes to stop
there, after all, for if he has no other title to
remembrance than his youth and death, then
his literary fame is but notoriety earned by
forgery.   If, on the other hand, there can be
discovered in what he wrote the clear promise
of a great performance in the future, then his
forgeries are a valuable part of our literature,
instead of being merely the wild error of an
ambitious boy, and his death becomes the
tragic end, not only of a young life, but of a
genius which, in its ripeness, might have given
joy to mankind.   To his writings, so well ed-
ited by Mr. Skeat some twenty years ago,
we must look for the answer to this question;
and they deserve examination, not only to

satisfy a curious inquiry, but for their own merits.*

Those merits, it must be confessed, have been disputed, and in at least one instance by one of the best of critics. In a notice of Edgar Poe, Mr. Lowell paused a moment to say that he "never thought the world lost more in the 'marvellous boy,' Chatterton, than a very ingenius imitator of antiquated dulness. When he becomes original (as it is called), the interest of ingenuity ceases and he becomes stupid." This uncompromising criticism always made me vaguely wonder whether the popular tradition or Mr. Lowell had estimated Chatterton rightly, for Mr. Lowell is very high authority, and he also had that exact knowledge, which is rarely the possession of those who make and repeat popular and accepted opinions. It is, in fact, hardly too much to suppose that the majority of possible readers, having a wholesome preference for their own tongue, have turned away affrighted at the hopeless jargon of Rowley, and taken what was said of Chatterton wholly on trust. No doubt it

---

* *The Poetical Works of Thomas Chatterton.* With an essay on the Rowley Poems by Walter Skeat, and a memoir by Edward Bell. London : George Bell & Sons. 1875.

is also true, as has just been said, that the
undeniably precocious powers of the boy, his
strange life and tragic death, have given a
fictitious interest, not only to him, but to his
unread works. Yet it must also be remembered that when Mr. Lowell gave his opinion,
neither he nor the world had had an opportunity to read Chatterton's poetry in an intelligible form, and so judge it fairly. This opportunity is given by Mr. Skeat. The "Rowleian
dialect," as Mr. Skeat calls it, was subjected
by him to a rigid examination, which resulted
in the discovery of the system upon which it
was formed. When this had been done, it then
became comparatively easy to translate the
poems and give them to the world in an intelligible version.

✓It appears that Chatterton, in the manufact-
ure of his dialect, proceeded in a simple way.
From Kersey's or Bailey's dictionary he copied
all the words marked O (old), with their meanings, in reverse order, into a manuscript book.
For instance, Kersey gives "cherisaunei (O)
—comfort," which would appear in the note-
book "comfort—cherisaunei." When a word
thus entered was susceptible of more than one
meaning, mistakes would be likely to occur.
For example, Kersey has "lissed (O)—bound-

ed," explained as "encircled by a list." This would be entered "bounded—lissed." Thus given, bounded might mean either surrounded by a list or leaped, and with the latter signification it is used several times by Chatterton. Another error of a somewhat different kind is curious. Kersey has "heck (O)—a rock," a misprint for rack. Chatterton uses it with its misprinted meaning of rock. Such mistakes, which abound, proved very important, for they furnished Mr. Skeat with conclusive proof of the correctness of his results. . Having thus got a foundation for his dialect, Chatterton enlarged it in three ways: by taking the groundwork of his word from Kersey and altering the termination, by altering the spelling of a word capriciously, and by coining words at pleasure, either from intelligible roots or from pure imagination. In the whole vocabulary there is found to be only seven per cent. of genuine old English words rightly used. The spelling is stolen entirely. It is the debased kind of "Chevy Chase," and the "Battle of Otterbourn." Mr. Skeat, after stating that a language on this system may be readily acquired in a few weeks, gives an amusing instance of the ease with which it may be applied:

" Offe mannes fyrste bykrous volunde wolle I singe
    And offe the fruite of yatte caltysned tre,
Whose lethal taste into thys worlde dydde brynge
    Both morthe and tene to all posteritie," etc.

The system and spelling were easy enough ;
the real difficulty was to supply the matter.
This Chatterton did, and then came the problem of editing him in such a way as to get at
the poems themselves. Four methods of solv-
ing this problem occurred to Mr. Skeat : to reprint the old text with old notes compiled
from former editions ; to reprint the old text
with sound critical notes ; to do away with
needless disguises of spelling, and reduce the
words to the sufficiently uniform spelling of
the fifteenth century ; or, finally, to do away
with needless disguises altogether, and, on the
correct theory of the poems not being genuine, render them into modern English. Of
the first method Mr. Skeat decided there had
been too much already ; that the second would
be a mere infliction on the reader ; and that
the third was absurd, as the poems were not
genuine, and in all cases, except where the language was practically modern English (as the
" Bristowe Tragedie "), such reduction would
have been impossible. The fourth method
proposed was therefore boldly taken, and the

poems, with a few exceptions, rendered into modern English. Oddly enough, the diction was improved by this translation and the rhythm rendered more melodious, indicating, as might have been conjectured, that Chatterton had written in eighteenth century English and translated into "Rowleian." I have sketched here only the results, but the ingenious processes employed to arrive at them well repay reading.

Thus, then, after a hundred years, the Rowley Poems were at last given to the world, stripped of all disguises, to stand or fall by their own merits. The work has proved to have been worth the labor expended on it by the editor. Passages of beauty which were hidden, together with a mass of bad lines, under the language of Rowley, are scattered through the poems. Even those familiar with Chatterton will pardon the quotation of a few lines in their modern form :

" When Autumn sere and sunburnt doth appear,
    With his gold hand gilding the falling leaf,
  Bringing up Winter to fulfil the year,
    Bearing upon his back the ripened sheaf ;
  When all the hills with woody seed are white,
  When lightning fires and gleams do meet from far
      the sight ;

" When the fair apples, red as evening sky,
    Do bend the tree unto the fruitful ground ;
When juicy pears, and berries of black dye
    Do dance in air, and call the eyes around ;
Then, be the evening foul or be it fair,
    Methinks my heart's delight is mingled with some
        care."

There are both feeling and imagination in these lines, uneven as they undoubtedly are in execution. The passage is taken from the " Tragedy of Ælla," a composition chiefly remarkable for its very weak construction and the absence of all dramatic elements. Yet among the feeble crudities of the poem there are indications, faint though they be, of passion and power in the following lines :

"*Æl.*—My better kindnesses which I did do,
 Thy gentleness doth represent so great,
 Like mighty elephants my gnats do shew ;
 Thou dost my thoughts of paying love abate.
 But had my actions stretched the roll of fate,
 Plucked thee from hell or brought heaven down
    to thee,
 Laid the whole world a footstool at thy feet,
 One smile would be sufficient meed for me.
 I am love's borrower, and can never pay,
 But be his borrower still and thine, my sweet,
    for aye."

In passing judgment on these lines, the extreme youth of the writer must be remembered. That Chatterton was little more than fifteen when he wrote this passage does much to atone for the obvious faults. Yet, besides its own merits, and beyond mere external resemblances, the poem has a distinct flavor of the great Elizabethan period. This quality is apparent in all the poems, and is of interest because it shows that the boy's instincts were true, and carried him back past the age of Anne to find his models in the great period of English literature.

"The Battle of Hastings," a long, dreary poem, containing a combat in each stanza, obviously written under Homeric influences, apparently exhibits nothing but Chatterton's unequalled power of spinning metred and rhymed lines. Yet, again, in all this waste of verses, we find on examination a long passage descriptive of "Kenewalcha Fair," which is a striking picture, and possesses beauty of imagery and language. After explaining who Kenewalcha was, the poet describes her as,

" White as the chalky cliffs of Britain's isle,
　　Red as the highest colored Gallic wine,
　Gay as all nature at the morning smile,
　　Those hues with pleasaunce on her lips combine ;

Her lips more red than summer evening skyen,
  Or Phœbus rising on a frosty morn;
Her breasts more white than snows in fields that
    lien,
  Or lily lambs that never have been shorn,
Swelling like bubbles in a boiling well,
Or new-burst brooklets gently whispering in the
    dell.

" Brown as the filbert dropping from the shell,
  Brown as the nappy ale at Hocktide game,
So brown the crooked rings that featly fell
  Over the neck of this all-beauteous dame.
Gray as the morn before the ruddy flame
  Of Phœbus' chariot rolling through the sky;
Gray as the steel-horned goats Conyan made tame,
  So gray appeared her featly sparkling eye;
Those eyes that oft did mickle pleased look
On Adhelm, valiant man, the virtues' doomsday-
    book.

" Majestic as the grove of oaks that stood
  Before the abbey built by Oswald king;
Majestic as Hibernia's holy wood,
  Where saints for souls departed masses sing;
Such awe from her sweet look forth issuing
  At once for reverence and love did call;
Sweet as the voice of thrushes in the spring,
  So sweet the words that from her lips did fall;
None fell in vain, all shewéd some intent;
Her wordés did display her great entendément.

" Taper as candles laid at Cuthbert's shrine,
  Taper as elms that Goodrick's abbey shrove,

Taper as silver chalices for wine,
  So taper were her arms and shapey-grove.
As skilful miners by the stones above
  Can ken what metal is contained below,
So Kenewalcha's face, y-made for love,
  The lovely image of her soul did show;
Thus was she outward formed; the sun, her mind,
Did gild her mortal shape, and all her charms re-
    fined."

No doubt these similes are many of them marked by youthful faults, and very grave faults too, yet such a one as

  "Gay as all nature at the morning smile,"

goes far to redeem other errors. These stanzas have been taken at random from many equally good and equally deserving examination. The excellences occur almost entirely in descriptive passages, as is certain to be the case with so young a writer, but it may fairly be said that there are indications of genius, or of something closely akin to it.

It is almost mere guess-work to attempt to fix Chatterton's real place among poets. It can, indeed, only be approximated very roughly by comparing his verses with other equally youthful productions. Tried by this test—and any other would be manifestly unjust—Chatterton comes out very well. The poetical blossoms of Cowley, long since withered, are insipid to the last degree, and the frigid morality of Pope's boyish performances is destitute of any real feeling. One is forced indeed to believe that the great poet of Queen Anne's reign was little better than a prig at the age of twelve. The " Hours of Idleness," Henry Kirke White's verses, the lispings of Moore, all these, and a host more, show nothing but an early capacity for smooth versification; and yet some of the writers came to great results and lasting fame afterwards. Shelley and Keats, who both wrote verse while very young, exhibit widely different powers from any of the men just mentioned. Despite the metaphysical speculations which disfigure "Queen Mab," passages of extraordinary beauty give no uncertain promise of the coming glories, while the sonnet on Chapman's Homer stands alone in its perfection among boyish productions and high up among the great sonnets of the language. Chatterton more nearly resembles Shelley than any of the others—not in quality or kind, but in the way in which his powers are shown. Apart from his marvellous fecundity, one finds buried in the mediæval débris passages of real beauty and strength both in thought and expression. The rarity of such qualities in juvenile verses entitles Chatterton to a high place among very young poets, and speculation may therefore fairly say that in the future —never reached—he might have been among the first. We agree with Mr. Lowell that the acknowledged, or "original," poetry was poor enough, and the reason is that the real poet was not there, but in the imaginary world which the boy had created for himself. Therefore it is that in the forgeries we find the imagination, the richness of diction, and the occasional beauty of thought which lift Chatterton up to a place as a poet, and which are almost wholly lacking in the other poems, where he was forcing himself to write without having his heart in his work.

In estimating Chatterton, it ought also to be taken into consideration that he did not form one of the regular links in the chain of literary development. He was sent into the world before his time. With the exception of Gray's splendid verse and a few poems by Collins and Goldsmith, it was a period of dust and ashes in poetry when Chatterton came upon the stage. The school of poetry which had been in its prime at the beginning of the century, was in the last stages of dissolution. It was commonly known as the didactic school of poetry, and how great it could be in its own way Pope had shown.   But the art of sinking in poetry had gone on rapidly since Pope's day, and it was reserved to the latter half of the same century to justify Canning's celebrated definition " that a didactic poem was so called from διδάσκειν, to teach, and ποίημα, a poem, because it teaches nothing and is not poetical."   No period of decline in literature is ever strong or fruitful, but the decadence of such a school as this was naturally more than usually barren.   Nature, under Queen Anne, was, at best, the pretty, trim nature of Windsor Forest ; in later days she became a painted, artificial creature, with not even youth to plead for her.   Against this nature of form and fashion Chatterton revolted.   From him comes the first lyric note, the harbinger of the great poetic outburst which was to uplift English poetry again at the end of that century and the beginning of the next.   But the world was not ready for him, and his voice fell upon deaf ears.   Chatterton's genius was imprisoned by conventionalities, and beat its wings wildly against the bars of the cage.   The only thing of beauty in the sluggish life of the dull provincial town was the ancient church of St. Mary. To this shrine the eager fancy of the boy turned and clung; here his genius and his aspirations found an outlet, and, repulsed by the every-day world, he was driven back into the dead world of the Middle Ages. The old church was a centre around which Chatterton's imagination wove a story; and in this fabric of his brain, and not in the dull years of Bristol or the fevered months of London, we find the real history of his life. The good burgher Canynge, the poet-priest Rowley and his friends, the knights and ladies at the tournaments, the inexorable king—these were the characters appearing in the romance which may be constructed from the poems. Here Chatterton was at home, here all was smiling and kindly. Horace Walpole might spurn him, but Rowley would not; and among the creatures of his fancy Chatterton found rest and peace, while outside all was harsh, bitter, and unsympathetic, with poverty for a companion and suicide for friend. To judge Chatterton as he was, we must go to the Rowley Poems, for there the real life was lived. In the weary years in Bristol, in the few short, mad months in London, the boy was acting a part. It is this distinction that makes the vast difference between the acknowledged and the Rowley Poems. Mr. Skeat follows Malone in thinking that the African Eclogues form the connecting link between the forgeries and the so-called genuine work. In this I cannot agree. They may be nearer than the others, but they are far, very far, from the poems of Rowley. In those alone do we find the promise of a worthy performance. The promise might never have been fulfilled, but nevertheless it is there. There, too, we can see the workings of an eager, passionate nature, creating for itself a realm of thought, where the boy lived his real life, more beautiful and more pathetic even than the history of his actual existence among men, which will always remain one of the great tragedies of English literature. It was the Rowley Poems, muffled in the clumsy and pitiful disguise under which their hapless author hoped they might steal their way to fame, which caused Wordsworth, with sure poetic instinct, to give to Chatterton his most enduring monument in the famous lines which have fixed him in our literature as

> " The marvellous boy,
> The sleepless soul that perished in his pride."

DR. HOLMES

DR. HOLMES

THE year which witnessed on the same day the birth of Abraham Lincoln and Charles Darwin seems to have a better right to be called *annus mirabilis* in the history of the English-speaking people than that year in the reign of Charles II., of blessed memory, which usually bears the title. But the great statesman and popular leader on one side of the Atlantic and the great man of science on the other were not the only gifts of 1809 to humanity. In that year were also born Gladstone and Tennyson and Oliver Wendell Holmes. A short time ago, perhaps, we might not have added the name of Dr. Holmes to this brief and memorable list. Death, however, changes and corrects the perspective wonderfully. Without any suggestion, or even thought, of comparisons, whether odious or the reverse, it is now easy to see that Dr. Holmes rightfully belongs among the remarkable men born in 1809. When he died, words were spoken about him in lands and languages not his own, which in a flash showed to all men, and especially to us of his own country, how large a place he had filled in this hurried and crowded world. Since then has come Mr. Morse's admirable biography, and that too adds to his fame and enables us to realize more clearly than ever before how great a space in literature Dr. Holmes occupied.

It is not my intention to trace the career of Dr. Holmes, for that has been done finally and in the most delightful manner by Mr. Morse. Dr. Johnson's hundred years, moreover, have only just begun, and it is too soon to say, "Come, let us judge him," but it is not too soon, perhaps, to look for a moment at the work he did and the place he filled, and to express our gratitude for both.

Dr. Holmes had in all ways a singularly happy and successful life. Literary fame came early and remained with him, ever growing and broadening. In his old age he did not have the sore trial of outliving his reputation, but saw it at the end as fresh and flourishing as in the beginning and with all the promise of long endurance. In Massachusetts, and especially in Boston, he was universally beloved,

and when it was known that he was dead, men
felt, despite his age, as if there, where he was
best known, his going made a gap in nature
and took from them something which was as
much a part of their being as the air they
breathed. Such a life, so full of happiness to
others and to himself, so crowded with all that
most men desire, may well be called fortunate.
Yet the word is not wholly apt or adequate.
Such a life is not all a matter of fortune. It
is in very large measure due to the man himself. Dr. Holmes owed his success to his own
gifts and to their wise use, but he also, in large
measure, owed the happiness which he both
enjoyed and imparted to his cheerful philosophy and to his wide, eager, and quick sympathies with all that touched mankind.

He was in one respect a very rare combination. He had the scientific mind, and at the
same time he was a poet and novelist. As a
physician, and as a lecturer for many years upon
anatomy, he won distinction and success, and
every form of scientific thought and inquiry had
for him always strong attractions. He could
think and could impart his knowledge with the
precision and accuracy which science demands.
Yet with this strongly marked habit of mind
were joined a lively imagination, the power to

body forth the shapes of things unknown, and
a most delicate fancy. These mental qualities
in a high degree of excellence are rarely found
together. Instances have not been wanting—
like Sir Thomas Browne, for example—of men
of scientific profession and training who had
likewise great literary gifts, and who as observ-
ers, thinkers, and writers take high rank. But
this is something very different from the genius
of the poet and romancer. The creative imagination and the scientific cast of thought, joined
as they were in Dr. Holmes, imply an extraordinary flexibility and versatility of mind. In
his case, too, the mingling of the different elements never affected either injuriously. Imagination did not make his medicine or anatomy
untrustworthy, nor did his scientific tendencies
make either his verse or his prose cold or dry.
His wit and humor, it is true, gleamed through
his lectures, and left behind them to a gener-
ation of students a rich harvest of stories and
traditions. The scientific cast of thought, on
the other hand, as it often supplied an image
or a metaphor, may possibly have had something to do also with the unfailing correctness
of the poet's verse. Certain at least it is that
the unusual combination of these widely differing qualities of mind was no less remarkable

than the fact that they never jarred upon each other, and never warped the life's work in either direction.

His fame, of course, was won as a man of letters, not as a man of science, and it is as a man of letters that the world at large looks upon him. Here his good fortune was with him also. He came at a good time. Before his birth, Jonathan Edwards, Benjamin Franklin, and Alexander Hamilton were the only American writers whose work had found a permanent place in literature. Two of these were specialists, one in theology, the other in statecraft, and both wrote with a particular purpose. Franklin alone had added to literature in its broad sense, and he, curiously enough, although neither a poet nor romancer, united great literary talent with scientific attainments of the highest order, as well as with the finest arts of the statesman and diplomatist. But one writer cannot create a literature, and it was left to the nineteenth century to show that Americans could make a distinct and characteristic contribution to the great literature of the English-speaking people.

Dr. Holmes's life covered the whole period of this literary development in which he was himself to play so large a part. *Knicker-*

bocker's History of New York, the first enduring work of this period, was finished in 1809,
the year of Dr. Holmes's birth. He was a
boy of six when "Thanatopsis" appeared, the
first poem of the new country which was to
hold a place in the higher poetry of our language. A few years later he might have read
Precaution, that pale imitation of an English
novel which Cooper sent forth to deserved failure, and then he could have rejoiced in the
series of American stories by the same author
which followed hard upon it, which added a
new figure to the great heroes of fiction, and
which travelled about the world with all the
delight of fresh adventure and original characters in their pages.

But while Dr. Holmes's birth and boyhood
were thus coincident with the appearance of
the earliest writings of Irving and Bryant and
Cooper, he himself and his own contemporaries were the men who were to do the largest
work for American literature in the century
just then beginning. Poe was born in the
same year as Holmes, and has himself a high
place in the list of the *annus mirabilis*. His
weak character and unhappy life obscured his
work and warped men's judgment, but his
wild genius has mounted steadily towards its

true place. He to whom so little was given in his lifetime has now, years after his death, called forth the admiration of English critics and excited the devotion of more than one French poet. At this moment a school of decadents and symbolists, who bear the same relation to our real literature that Lyly, with his " Euphues," bore to the literature of the Elizabethans, find, as they think, in Poe, who is real and lasting, a master and forerunner, as well as a justification for their own little passing fashion.

But Poe stood far apart from the men with whom Dr. Holmes is inseparably connected. Hawthorne, the greatest of them all in a purely literary sense, was only four years Holmes's senior. Emerson was born in 1803, Longfellow in 1807, Whittier in 1808. Lowell, who was, perhaps, more intimate with Dr. Holmes than any one else, was only ten years his junior, while the historians, Bancroft and Prescott, Motley and Parkman, were his life-long friends and comrades in greater or less degree. They were all New Englanders, all offspring of the old Puritan stock. It was a remarkable group of men; and now that the last has gone we can see what a large place they fill in American literature, and how much of all that we like to think of as lasting in that literature is their work. Poe, who did not love them, and who felt that they did not appreciate the genius which he knew himself to possess, was wont to rail at them as the "New England school." Some of his keen criticism of them and others was both true and penetrating, but he was wrong when he called these men "a school." They were in no sense "a school," for they differed as utterly in their work as they did in their purposes and lines of thought. They may have shared certain literary opinions and they were undoubtedly friends, but "a school" cannot exist without teachers and pupils, leaders and followers, and these men were equals, working each in his own way.

Of all the group, Dr. Holmes, although he may not hold the highest place among them for literary achievement, was the most various in performance and the most versatile in faculty. We all think of him first as a poet. There are some of his poems which are in every one's mind, which live in our memories, and rise to our lips. In a recent notice in some English journal, it was said, with a faint flavor of patronage, that certain of Dr. Holmes's poems were in all the anthologies. The critic might have added that most good poems in the language are. To say of a poet that his verses are in all the anthologies, and on the lips of the people, has been a noble praise from the days of Tyrtæus to our own. Dr. Holmes has won this place. Certain of his poems, like " The Chambered Nautilus," " The Last Leaf," or "Old Ironsides," are in every collection. They have passed into our speech, they have become part of our inheritance ; and greater assurance of remembrance than this no man can have.

Dr. Holmes is perhaps thought of most often as the poet of occasion, and certainly no one has ever surpassed him in this field. He was always apt, always happy ; he always had the essential lightness of touch, and the right mingling of wit and sentiment. But he was very much more than a writer of occasional verse, and his extraordinary success in this direction has tended to obscure his much higher successes, and to cause men to overlook the fact that he was a true poet in the best sense. The brilliant occasional poems were only the glitter on the surface of the stream, while behind and beneath them lay depths of feeling and beauties of imagery and thought to which full justice has not yet been, but surely will be, done. ˙He felt this a little

10

himself; and he never wrote a truer line than
when he said :

"While my gay stanza pleased the banquet's lords,
  My soul within was tuned to deeper chords."

In his poetry and in his mastery of all the
forms of verse, he showed the variety of talent which was perhaps his most characteristic
quality.   He had a strong bent towards that
kind of poetry of which Pope is the best example, and he possessed much in common
with the author of the *Essay on Man*.   He
had the same easy flow in his verse, the same
finish, wit of a kindlier sort, the same wisdom
without any attempt at rhymed metaphysics,
and a like power of saying, in smooth and perfect lines,

" What oft was thought, but ne'er so well expressed."

The metrical form which is so identified with
Pope always seemed to appeal to Dr. Holmes,
and, when he employed it, it lost nothing in
his hands.   But this was only one of many in-
struments he used.   He was admirable in narrative and ballad poetry, the poetry of energy,
movement, and incident, of which "Bunker Hill
Battle" is as good an example as any.   He

ventured often into the dangerous domain of
comic poetry, where so few have succeeded
and so many failed, and he always came out
successful, saved by the sanity and balance
which one always feels in everything he wrote.
Of a much higher order were the poems of dry
humor, where a kindly satire and homely wisdom pointed the moral, as in the "One Hoss
Shay." But he did work far finer and better
than all this, excellent as this was in its kind.
He was not one of

>   "The bards sublime,
> Whose distant footsteps echo through the corridors
>   of time."

Nor was he one of those who seem to have
sounded all the depths and shoals of passion.
I do not think he thought so himself or ever
was under the least misapprehension as to the
nature of his own work, and in this freedom
from illusions lay one secret of his success and
of the tact which never failed. I remember his
saying to me in speaking of orators and writers, that once or twice in the lives of such men
there came a time when they did, in the boy's
phrase, "a little better than they knew how."
I naturally asked if such a moment had ever
come to him. He smiled, and I well recall

his reply: "Yes, I think in the 'Chambered Nautilus' I may have done a little 'better than I knew how.'" There can be no doubt that in that beautiful poem, which we all know by heart, there is a note of noble aspiration which is found only in the best work. But that is not the only one by any means. That same aspiring note is often heard in his verse, and there are many poems by Dr. Holmes filled with the purest and tenderest sentiment. Such, for instance, are the lines on the death of his classmate and friend, Professor Peirce; such, also, is the "Iron Gate," the tender and beautiful poem which he read at the breakfast given him on his seventieth birthday. Such, too, are his lyrics, which include much of his best work, and which have in a high degree the fervor and the concentration which the best lyric ought always to possess.

People generally link his name with a memory of wit and humor, for he had both in large measure, and the world is very grateful to any one who can make it laugh. But the sentiment and aspiration, which are of higher quality than wit and humor can ever be, and which are felt most often in the poems that love of man or love of country have inspired, as well as the perfection of the poet's workmanship and the originality of his thought, are in Dr. Holmes too often overlooked. This perfection of form and felicity of imagery never left him. In the poem on the death of Francis Parkman, written only a year before his own death, when he was well past eighty, there is neither weakness nor falling off. The sentiment is as true and simple as ever, the flow of the verse as easy, and when he puts England's conquest of France in Canada into the single line

"The Lilies withered where the Lion trod,"

we need no critic to tell us that the old happiness of phrase and power of imagery remained undimmed to the last.

Yet, when all is said of his poetry, of which he left so much fixed in our language to be prized and loved and remembered, I think it cannot be doubted that the work of Dr. Holmes which will be most lasting is to be found in the *Autocrat of the Breakfast Table* and its successors. The novel of *Elsie Venner* is a strong and interesting book. The story holds us fast, and the study of a strange and morbid state of mind has the fascination given to the snakes themselves. Such a book would have made the fame and fortune of a lesser man. But, as lasting literature in the highest sense, it falls behind the *Autocrat*. There the whole man spoke. There he found full scope for his wit and humor and mirth, his keen observation, his varied learning, his worldly wisdom, his indignation with wrong, and his tenderest sentiment. To attempt to analyze the *Autocrat* and its successors would be impossible. It is not the kind of literature that lends itself to analysis or criticism. It is the study of many-sided humanity in the form of the essay rather than the novel, although the creation and development of character play in it a large part. Such books, with the quality of enduring life, are few and rare, although many have attempted them, but when they really have the vital qualities they are not of the fashion of the day which passeth away, but for all time, because they open to us the pages of the great book of human nature. Montaigne and Addison, Goldsmith, Sterne, and Charles Lamb are the best, perhaps the only masters really in this field, for the exact combination of wit and humor, of pathos and wisdom, of sense and sentiment, where the lesson of life runs close beneath the jest and the realities tread hard upon the fancies, is as essential as it is rare. To this small and chosen company Dr. Holmes belongs, and in it he holds high place. All the qualities, all the diversities are there, and, most important of all, the perfect balance among them is there too. The style runs with the theme, always easy but never slovenly, always pure and good but never labored, like talk by the fireside, without either affectation or carelessness, while over it all (and this is stronger in Dr. Holmes than in any one else) hangs an atmosphere of friendliness which draws us nearer to the writer than any other quality. Writings such as these have all had, perhaps all require, the air of learning as evidence that to keen observation of man has been added the knowledge of many books. It is to be feared that Sterne, sham as he was for all his genius, got his learning by wholesale theft from Burton. But the learning of the others was genuine, and in no one more so than in Dr. Holmes. He had an eager love of knowledge of all kinds, whether new or old, which carried him far afield. Like Dr. Johnson, he rarely read a book through from cover to cover, but also like Dr. Johnson, he absorbed all there was in a book with great quickness and remarkable power of retention. He has said in print, I believe—I remember certainly his saying to me—that two of the

books which he always kept by him for odd
moments or the wakeful hours were Montaigne
and Burton. It was a most typical choice : the
Frenchman of olden time looking out on life
with his keen vision and cheerful cynicism, and
the melancholy Englishman with his curious
and rambling learning strongly tinctured with
quaint medical lore. Dr. Holmes, who loved
them both, ranged over the fields that both
had occupied, as well as over others they had
never touched.

It is in his novels, to which I have only allud-
ed, that the critics have agreed that Dr. Holmes
had least success. So far as *Elsie Venner* is
concerned, I am not of this mind. But it is
generally overlooked that in the *Autocrat* and
its successors he has drawn and created characters which all his readers love and remember, and that he has also described in these
same volumes little scenes and situations which
show the best art of the novelist. Let me
quote a single example, the familiar scene of
the " Long Path " on Boston Common, in the
Autocrat :

" At last I got out the question—' Will you take the
long path ?' ' Certainly,' said the school-mistress, ' with
much pleasure.' ' Think,' I said, ' before you answer ;
if you take the long path with me now, I shall in-

terpret it that we shall part no more.' The school-
mistress stepped back with a sudden movement as if
an arrow had struck her.

"One of the long granite blocks used as seats was
hard by—the one you may still see close by the Gingko
tree. 'Pray sit down,' I said. 'No, no,' she answered,
softly, 'I will walk the long path with you.'"

Surely there is a very beautiful, a very
charming art in this little scene. It is as
good as the death of Lefevre in *Tristram
Shandy*, and has much the same qualities of
tenderness and reserve, of simplicity and suggestion.

I have spoken very inadequately of the writer, not at all of the man. It is not easy for
those of us who have known Dr. Holmes all
our lives and who have lived so near to him, to
write of him with the proper critical discrim-
ination. The spell is yet upon us, the charm
is still too potent. We have the personal
feeling too strongly with us to be entirely dis-
passionate as judges or critics of the man himself.

But Dr. Holmes had one personal quality
which ought not to be passed over without
mention anywhere or at any time. He was a
thorough American and always a patriot, always national and independent, and never co-

lonial or cosmopolitan or subservient to foreign opinion. In the war of the rebellion no one was a stronger upholder of the national cause than he. In his earliest verse we catch constantly the flutter of the flag, and in his war poems we feel the rush and life of the great uprising which saved the nation. He was in the best sense a citizen of the world, of broad and catholic sympathies. But he was first and before that an American, and this fact is at once proof and reason that he was able to do work which has carried delight to many people of many tongues, and which has won him a high and lasting place in the great literature of the English-speaking people as well as among that small and beloved company of authors with whom we like to live and talk, and who are, above all things else, our familiar friends.

A LIBERAL EDUCATION

A LIBERAL EDUCATION *

THE most splendid chapter in modern history is that which tells of the rise of the new learning in Europe and in England. It has all the unspeakable charm of spring, and all the glory of awakening life which Michael Angelo drew on the vaulting of the Sistine Chapel and called the creation of Adam. Men struggled up out of the darkness of the Middle Ages with much sore labor. That they won through as they did was due to men's bringing up from their hiding places all that was left of the writings and the art of Rome and Greece. In the fragments of these two great literatures were revealed the thought, the art, and the history of a high and long-forgotten civilization. The discovery roused the intellect of Europe from its long sleep. For centuries this awakening was called the revival of

* An address delivered before the Phi Beta Kappa Society of Harvard University, in Sanders Theatre, Thursday, June 28, 1894.

learning; and the burst of genius in literature and art and thought, which followed hard upon it, has never been equalled in richness of production or in exuberance of life. Small wonder is it that mankind felt a profound gratitude to the literatures which had thus led them to the light. It was natural enough that under such conditions they should have looked upon learning as a knowledge of the classics, and should have defined a classical as a liberal education.

✓Thus it came to pass that a liberally educated man was one educated in the classics, and a man who did not know the classics, no matter what his other acquirements might be, stood without the sacred pale. This definition of a liberal education has lasted to our own time, and technically it is still correct. Yet we all know that there has been a widespread revolt in practice from the old and classic theory. To my thinking, the pendulum has now swung too far. Mere knowledge of the Latin and Greek literatures no longer makes nor can make a liberal education, but Greek and Latin nevertheless ought invariably to be a part of it. To read Greek and Latin is always, and at the very least, an accomplishment and a refinement. The key which opens the door to the Iliad should be forced into the hand of every boy seeking the higher education. Then we may part company with the old system, if you will, and let the student turn the key or leave the door locked, as he pleases. But so far as the threshold, at least, of those great poems, the old and the new theories ought to travel together.

I have, however, no intention of entering upon the well-fought ground of the study of the classics. My purpose here is very different. It is to speak of a liberal education in its broadest and truest sense, without any reference to recent controversies over the study of what are misnamed the dead languages, just as if the speech of Homer could ever die while civilization lives. To understand, however, the real relation of a liberal education to our American life, the first step is a right definition. We all know the conventional or classical definition, but we must have the true one as well.

One of the best known and least read of Queen Anne's men is Sir Richard Steele. His good and evil fortune, his kind heart, his ready wit, his attractive but somewhat imperfect character, are all familiar to a large posterity with whom he has ever been popular. But his writings, in which he took so much simple pride, are, it is to be feared, largely unread. The book of quotations contains only two sentences of his writing, and one of these can hardly be called familiar. But the other fully deserves the adjective, for it is perhaps the finest compliment ever paid by a man to a woman. Steele wrote of Lady Elizabeth Hastings that "to love her was a liberal education," and thus rescued her forever from the oblivion of the British Peerage. He certainly did not mean by this that to love the Lady Elizabeth was as good as a knowledge of Latin and Greek, for that would have been no compliment at all, unless from Carlyle's friend Dryasdust, a very different personage from the gallant and impecunious husband of "Prue." No, Steele meant something very far removed from Latin and Greek, and everybody knows what he meant, even if one cannot put it readily into words.

To the mind of the eighteenth century, a liberal education entirely classical, if you please, so far as books went, meant the education which bred tolerance and good manners and courage, which taught a man to love honor and truth and patriotism, and all things of good report. Like the history of Sir John Froissart, it was the part of a liberal education "to encourage all valorous hearts and to show them honorable examples." Such, I think, we all believe a liberal education to be to-day, in its finest and best sense. But yet this is not all, nor are the fields of learning which a great university opens to its students all. Besides the liberal education of Steele and the ample page of knowledge which a university unrolls, there is still something more, and this something is the most important part.

The first expression that we get as to the purposes of our own university is given in *New England's First Fruits*, published in London in 1643. It is there said: "One of the next things we longed for, and looked after, was to advance learning and perpetuate it to posterity; dreading to leave an illiterate ministry to the churches when our present ministers shall lie in the dust."

The later charters of the college all proposed as its purpose that it should fit persons for the church and for civil employment, and in these old phrases is the kernel of the whole matter. It was the object of the college, as the Puritans looked at it, to perpetuate learning, which was at once the badge and guide of civilization, but it was also and equally the object of the college to fit its students for life.

11

The founders of the college mentioned only one field of work, that of the ministry. It was a natural limitation enough at that time. The clergy were the most powerful, and to the Puritan mind by far the most important, class in the community, and therefore this early account of New England tells us that the leading object of the college was to maintain a learned ministry. Fifty years later the views had widened, and the purpose of the college is then defined as the preparation of men not only for the church, but for civil employment, or, in other words, for the service of the State. This idea has gone on broadening ever since, until now the true conception of the highest duty of a great university is, or ought to be, to fit its scholars for the life which lies before them when they go out into the world. Ordinarily we think of a college simply as a place where men receive their preliminary training for the learned professions, where they lay the foundations for a life of scientific or historical investigation, for classical scholarship, or for the study of modern languages or literature, and where they gather that general knowledge which constitutes the higher education, even if the student leaves learning behind him at the college gate to enter on a life of action or of business. Yet in reality these are but the details of a liberal education, and we do not want to lose sight of the city on account of the number of houses immediately around us.

The first and the most important function of a liberal education is to fit a man for the life before him, and to prepare him, whatever profession or pursuit he may follow, to be a useful citizen of the country which gave him birth. This is of vast importance in any country, but in the United States it is of peculiar moment, because here every man has imposed upon him the duties of sovereignty, and in proportion to his capacity and his opportunities are the responsibilities of that sovereignty.

A liberal education is a great gift and a high privilege. Every one who is fortunate enough to receive it ought to realize what it has cost. Many men obtain it in the most honorable manner by great personal effort, self-sacrifice, and self-control. They are sure to value it aright. But the cost to which I refer is greater than this. These vast endowments which have founded and built up American colleges, from the noble and often pathetic gifts of the early settlers down to the millions which have been given in our own time, represent the devotion, the ambition, the toil, and the thrift of thousands of men and women who have sought to do something according to their strength, that those who came after them might have more generous opportunities, and that civilization might be advanced. Thus it is that a liberal education is such a precious and dearly bought gift to those who obtain it. Yet it is not enough even that the men who receive a liberal education should appreciate it. It is far more important that the universities which dispense it should understand what it means in its widest sense, and should direct it to its true purposes; for it is possible so to pervert it that it shall be of no value, but rather an injury, not only to the student but to the community, and in this wise become hurtful to education itself.

If a man is not a good citizen it boots little whether he is a learned Grecian or a sound Latinist. If he is out of sympathy with his country, his people, and his time, the last refinement and the highest accomplishments are of slight moment. But it is of the utmost importance that every man, and especially every educated man, in the United States, no matter what his profession or business, should be in sympathy with his country, with its history in

the past, its needs in the present, and its aspirations for the future. If he has this, all the
rest will follow, and it is precisely at this point
that there seems to be a real danger in our university life and in our liberal education. The
peril, moreover, is none the less real because
the wrong influence is subtle.

We are apt to gather here at the end of
each college year in a kindly and very natural spirit of mutual admiration. Those of
us who come from the busy outside world,
come to renew old memories, and to brighten,
if only for a moment, the friendships which
time and separation would darken and rust.
We are in no mood for criticism. Yet it is
perhaps as well not to let the mutual con-
gratulations go too far, for we have the advantage of coming from without, and are not
likely to mistake the atmosphere which gath-
ers about a university for that of the world at
large. A lord chancellor of England said some
years ago, in a speech in Balliol College hall,
"I am glad to be informed from preceding
speakers of the talents, virtues, and distinction
of the company here present. Would that I
were fifty years younger to be educated under
such influences as these. Had I that good
fortune there is no knowing what I should

become. It is owing to men like these that Oxford can boast that the tide of civilization flows within her limits, lower, indeed, but not much lower than in the world around." Some people may be heretics enough to think that similar observation might not be out of place sometimes as a suggestion at least at the commencement dinners of some of our own universities. In any event, the sting of the lord chancellor's satire lay as usual in its large leaven of truth. The danger of every university lies in its losing touch with the world about it. This is bad anywhere. It is worse in a republic than anywhere else.

We must, however, be more definite again if we would reach any result. "Losing touch" is a vague expression; "lack of sympathy" is little better. It is not easy to put my meaning in one word, but perhaps to say that the first duty of an American university and its liberal education should be to make its students good Americans comes as near to it as anything. Still we must go a step further, for many persons are prone to sneer at the demand for Americanism, as if it meant merely a blatant and boastful Chauvinism, employed only for the baser political uses. There is always an attempt to treat it as if

it were something like the utterances which
Dickens satirized long ago in the persons of
Jefferson Brick and Elijah Pogram. That was
certainly neither an agreeable nor creditable
form of national self-assertion. Yet it was infinitely better, coarse and boastful as it was,
than the opposite spirit which turns disdainfully even from the glories of nature because
they are American and not foreign, and which
looks scornfully at the Sierras because they
are not the Alps. The Bricks and the Po-
grams may have been coarse and vulgar, yet
the spirit of which they were caricatures was
at least strong, and capable of better things,
while the other spirit is pitifully weak, and
has no future before it except one of further
decay.

True Americanism is something widely different from either of these. It is really only
another word for intelligent patriotism. Loud
self-assertion has no part in it, and mere criticism and carping, with their everlasting whine
because we are not as others are, cannot exist
beside it. Americanism in its right sense does
not tend in the least to repress wholesome
criticism of what is wrong; on the contrary, it
encourages it. But this is the criticism which
is made only as the first step towards a rem-

edy, and is not mere snarling for snarling's
sake. Such Americanism as this takes pride
in what we have done and in the men we
have bred, and knows not the eternal comparison with other people which is the sure
sign of a tremulous little mind, and of a deep
doubt of one's own position.

To all which the answer is constantly made
that this is merely asserting a truism and a
commonplace, and that of course every one
is intelligently patriotic. Of the great mass
of our people this is true beyond question.
They are thoroughly patriotic in the best
sense. Theoretically it is true of all. Practically there is still much left to be desired
among our liberally educated men, and it is of
this precise defect among those who have a
liberal education that I wish to speak.

The danger of the higher education of a
great university is, that in widening the hori-
zon it may destroy the sense of proportion so
far as our own country is concerned. The
teachings of a university open to us the literature, the art, the science, the learning, and the
history of all other nations. They would be
quite worthless if they did not do so. These
teachings form, and necessarily form, the great
mass of all that we study here. That which

relates to our own country is inevitably only a small part, comparatively speaking, of the great whole. This also is quite natural. Our own nation is comparatively new. Its history is not long, and it is not set off by the glitter of a court, or of an ancient aristocracy. Our literature is young. Our art is just developing. In the broad sweep of a liberal education, that portion which relates to the United States is but one of many parts. Hence there is a tendency to lose the sense of proportion, to underrate our own place in the history and life of the world, and to forget that knowledge of our own country, while it excludes nothing else, is nevertheless more important to each one of us than that of all other countries, if we mean to play a man's part in life. There is no danger that liberally educated men will overvalue their own country; there is great danger that they will undervalue it. This does not arise from any lack of opportunity here to learn our history, or to know what we have done as a people. It comes from a failure rightly to appreciate our history and our achievements. We are too apt to think of ourselves as something apart and inferior, and to fail to see our true place in the scale of nations. Many men of liberal education either expect too much of the United States, or value too little what has been accomplished here. As has just been said, we are a young nation—and certain fruits of a high civilization require time to ripen. It is foolish to criticise the absence of those things which time alone can bring to perfection, and their coming is retarded, not hastened, by fault-finding. On the other hand, we are apt to overlook what really has been done, and we often fail to judge rightly because we use superficial comparisons with some other contemporary people, instead of measuring ourselves by the just standards of the world's history.

Let us look for a moment at the last hundred years which cover our history as a nation. In that time we have conquered a continent, won it from the wilderness and the savages, by much privation, and much desperate and heroic fighting, unrecorded for the most part, with nature and with man. Where else in the nineteenth century will you find such a conquest as that? And this empire that we have conquered we have saved also from being rent asunder. That work of salvation cost us four years of war. Look again over the nineteenth century and see where you can find a war of like magnitude, equal to ours in its stake, its fighting, its sacrifices, or in the noble spirit that it evoked among our people. As the French traveller said, standing among the graves at Arlington, "Only a great people is capable of a great civil war."

I will not touch upon the material development, unequalled in history, which has gone hand in hand with this conquest of waste places and fighting tribes of Indians. It is enough here to count only those higher things which show the real greatness of a nation.

Turn to the men. In our hundred years we have given to the world's roll of statesmen Washington and Lincoln. You cannot match them elsewhere in the same period. Are there any better or purer or greater than they to be found in the tide of time? Take up the list of great soldiers. Setting aside Napoleon, who stands all apart with Cæsar and Hannibal, what nation has made a larger gift to the leaders of men in battle than the country which added to the list the names of Washington, Grant, and Lee? Since Nelson fell at Trafalgar, where in naval warfare will you find a greater chief than Farragut?

In those wonderful inventions which have affected the history and development of man, the country which has given to the world the cotton-gin, the telegraph, the sewing-machine, the steamship, the telephone, and the armored ship holds a place second to none.

Turn now to those fields which exact the conditions of an old civilization—wealth, leisure, and traditions.   Even here, despite the adverse circumstances of national youth, there is much to record, much to give fair promise, much in which to rejoice.

From the time of Franklin and his kite, we ever have done our share in scientific work. We have developed a literature of our own, and made it part of the great literature of the English-speaking race.   The Luxembourg has opened its jealously guarded doors to give space and place to five American painters, and the chisel of St. Gaudens has carved statues which no contemporary elsewhere can rival. The buildings at the Chicago Fair came as a beautiful surprise and a great achievement. They showed that we had the capacity to take rank among the great building races of the earth.

It is a great record for a hundred years. Even if we glance only at the mountain tops, it is a remarkable story of conquest and growth. If our universities do not teach us to value it rightly they are of little worth, for to know the present and to act in it we must have a just knowledge of our place in history. If we have that knowledge, we shall realize that a nation which, whatever its shortcomings, has done so much and bred such men, has a promise for the future and a place in the world which brings a grave responsibility to those who come to the inheritance.

The first step, then, for our universities, if in the true spirit of a liberal education they seek to fit men for the life about them, is to make them Americans and send them forth in sympathy with their country. And the second step is like the first: A university should aim to put a man in sympathy with his time, and make him comprehend it, if we would have him take effective part in the life of his time. As the danger on the first point of patriotism is that the many-sided teachings of a university will prevent a just sense of the place held by our country, so on the second point the danger is that dealing largely with the past, the university will alienate its students from the present. The past is a good schoolhouse but a bad dwelling-place. We cannot really understand the present without the fullest knowledge of the past, but it is the present with which we are to deal, and the past must not be allowed to hide it.

There is a visible tendency in universities
to become in their teachings *laudatores tem-
poris acti*, and this tendency is full of peril.
The world was never made better, the great
march of humanity was never led by men
whose eyes were fixed upon the past. The
leaders of men are those who look forward,
not backward.

> "For not through eastern windows only,
>   When daylight comes, comes in the light;
> In front the sun climbs slow, how slowly,
>   But westward look—the land is bright."

As I say do not undervalue your own country, so I say do not undervalue your own
time. The nineteenth century is dying. It
has been a great century. It has seen Water-
loo and Sedan and Gettysburg. As it has
passed along it has beheld the settlement of
Australia and South Africa, and the conquest
of the American continent. It has replaced
the stage-coach with the locomotive, and
united the continents with electric cables. It
has been the century of Lincoln and Bismarck,
of Wellington and Grant, and Lee and Moltke.
Scott and Thackeray, Dickens and Hawthorne
have woven stories to rejoice it; and Browning and Tennyson and Victor Hugo, Lowell

and Poe have been among its later poets. It
has been a time richly worth living in. Now
in its closing years, with the new and unknown century hard upon us, it is more than
ever a time worth living in, full of marvellous
voices to those who will listen with attentive
ears, full of opportunity to any one who will
take part in its strifes, fullest of all of profound interest to those who will look upon it
with considerate eyes.

How, then, is a university to reach the results we ought to have from its teachings in
this country and this period? How is it to
inspire its students with sympathy for their
country and their time as the most important
of all its lessons? Some persons may reply
that it can be obtained by making the university training more practical. Much has
been said on this point first and last, but the
theory, which is vague at best, seems to me
to have no bearing here. It is not a practical
education which we seek in this regard, even
if it was the business of a university to give
one, but a liberal education, which shall foster
certain strong qualities of heart and head.
Our search now and here is not for an education which shall enable a man to earn his living with the least possible delay, but for a

training which shall develop character and mind along certain lines.

To one man Harvard gives the teaching which fits him to be an engineer; to another, that which opens to him law or medicine or theology. But to all her students alike it is her duty to give that which will send them out from her gates able to understand and to sympathize with the life of the time. This cannot be done by rules or systems or text-books. It can come, and can only come, from the subtle, impalpable, and yet powerful influences which the spirit and atmosphere of a great university can exert upon those within its care. It is not easy to define or classify those influences, although we all know their general effect. Nevertheless it is, I think, possible to get at something sufficiently definite to indicate what is lacking, and where the peril lies. It all turns on the spirit which inspires the entire collegiate body, on the mental attitude of the university as a whole. This brings us at once to the danger which I think confronts all our large universities to-day, and which I am sure confronts that university which I know and love best. We are given over too much to the critical spirit, and we are educating men to become critics of

other men, instead of doers of deeds themselves. This is all wrong. Criticism is health-
ful, necessary, and desirable, but it is always
abundant, and is infinitely less important than
performance. There is not the slightest risk
that the supply of critics will run out, for
there are always enough middle-aged failures
to keep the ranks full, if every other resource
should fail. But even if we were short of
critics, it is a sad mistake to educate young
men to be mere critics at the outset of life.
It should be the first duty of a university to
breed in them far other qualities. Faith, hope
and belief, enthusiasm and courage are the
qualities to be trained and developed in
young men by a liberal education. Youth is
the time for action and for work, not for criticism. A liberal education should encourage
the spirit of action, not deaden it. We want
the men whom we send out from our universities to count in the battle of life and in the
history of their time, and to count more and
not less because of their liberal education.
They will not count at all, be well assured, if
they come out trained only to look coldly
and critically on all that is being done in the
world, and on all who are doing it. Long
ago Emerson pointed the finger of scorn at

12

this type when he said: "There is my fine young Oxford gentleman, who says there is nothing new and nothing true and no matter." We cannot afford to have that type, and it is the true product of that critical spirit which says to its scholars, "See how badly the world is governed; see how covered with dust and sweat the men are who are trying to do the world's business, and how many mistakes they make; let us sit here in the shade with Amaryllis and add up the errors of these bruised, grimy fellows, and point out what they ought to do, while we make no mistakes ourselves by sticking to the safe rule of attempting nothing." This is a very comfortable attitude, but it is the one of all others which a university should discourage instead of inculcating. Moreover, with such an attitude of mind towards the world of thought and action is always allied a cultivated indifference, than which there is nothing more enervating.

And these things are no pale abstractions because they are in their nature purely matters of sentiment and thought. When Cromwell demanded the New Model, he said, "A set of poor tapsters and town apprentices would never fight against men of honor."

They were of the same race and the same
blood as the cavaliers, these tapsters and apprentices; they had the same muscles and the
same bodily form and strength. It was the
right spirit that was lacking, and this Cromwell, with the keen eye of genius, plainly saw.
So he set against the passion of loyalty the
stern enthusiasm of religion, and swept resistance from his path. One sentiment against
another, and the mightier conquered. Come
nearer to our own time. Some six thousand
ill-armed American frontiersmen met ten thousand of the unconquered army of Wellington's
veterans hard by New Orleans. They beat
them in a night attack, they got the better of
them in an artillery duel, and finally they drove
back with heavy slaughter the onset of these
disciplined troops who had over and over again
carried by storm defences manned by the soldiers of Napoleon. These backwoodsmen
were of the same race as their opponents, no
stronger, no more inured to hardships than
Wellington's men, but they had the right
spirit in them. They did not stop to criticise the works, and to point out that cotton-
bales were not the kind of rampart recognized
in Europe. They did not pause to say that a
properly constituted army ought to have bayo-

nets and that they had none. Still less did they set about finding fault with their leader. They went in and did their best, and their best was victory. One example is as good as a hundred. It is the spirit, the faith, the courage, the determination of men which have made the world move. These are the qualities which have carried the dominion of the English-speaking people across continents and over wide oceans to the very ends of the earth. It is the same in every field of human activity. The men who see nothing but the lions in the path, who fear ridicule and dread mistakes, who behold the faults they may commit more plainly than the guerdon to be won, win no battles, govern no states, write no books, carve no statues, paint no pictures. The men who do not fear to fall are those who rise. It is the men who take the risks of failure and mistakes who win through defeats to victory.

If the critical spirit govern in youth, it chokes action at its very source. We must have enthusiasm, not indifference; willingness to subordinate ourselves to our purpose, if we would reach results, and an imperfect result is far better than none at all. Abraham Lincoln said once, speaking of Henry Clay, "A free people in times of peace and quiet, when

pressed by no common danger, naturally divide into parties. /At such times the man who
is of neither party is not, cannot be, of any
consequence./ Mr. Clay was therefore of a
party." This which Lincoln said of politics
merely expresses in a single direction the truth
that a man cannot succeed who is a mere critic.
(He must have the faith and enthusiasm which
will enable him to do battle whether with sword
or pen, with action or thought, for a cause in
which he believes.) This does not imply any
lack of independence, any blind subservience
to authority or prejudice. Far from it. But
it does imply the absence of the purely critical
spirit with no purpose but criticism, which dries
up the very springs of action.

> "That is the doctrine simple, ancient, true;
>   Such is life's trial, as old Earth smiles and knows.
>   Make the low nature better by your throes;
>   Give earth yourself, go up for gain above."

There is nothing fanciful in all this. It is
very real, very near, very practical. You cannot win a boat-race, or a football-match unless
you have the right spirit. Thews and sinews
are common enough. They can be had for the
asking. But the best will not avail if they are
not informed with the right spirit. You must

have more than trained muscles; you must
have enthusiasm, determination, brains, and
the capacity for organization and subordina-
tion.   If the critical spirit prevails, and every
one is engaged in criticising, analyzing, and declaring how much better things would be if
they were only different from what they are,
you will not, you cannot, win, other things
being equal.   Differences in physical qualities
may often determine results, but such differences come and go like luck at a game of cards.
But if the critical, indifferent spirit reigns, it
means sure and continued defeats, for it saps
the very roots of action and success.

As it is in the struggles of the playground
or the river, so it is in the wider fields of serious life.   If the college merely teaches young
men to tell the truth and keep their hands
clean, they have learned two lessons which are
very valuable each in its own way.   But if this
be all, the result of the teaching will be many
gentlemanly failures and comparatively few
successful men.   If a university breeds a race
of little critics, they will be able to point out
other men's faults and failures with neatness
and exactness, but they will accomplish nothing themselves.   They will make the world no
better for their presence, they will not count

in the conflict, they will not cure a single one
of the evils they are so keen to detect. Worst
of all, they will bring reproach on a liberal education, which will seem to other men to be a
hinderance when it should be a help.

The time in which we live is full of questions of the deepest moment. There has
been, during the century now ending, the
greatest material development ever seen—
greater than that of all preceding centuries together. The condition of the average man
has been raised higher than ever before, and
wealth has been piled up beyond the wildest
fancy of romance. We have built up a vast
social and industrial system, and have carried
civilization to the highest point it has ever
touched. That system and that civilization
are on trial. Grave doubts and perils beset
them. The economic theories of fifty years
ago stand helpless and decrepit in their immo-
bility before the social questions which face
us now. Everywhere to-day there is an om-
inous spirit of unrest. Everywhere there is
a feeling that all is not well when wealth
abounds and none the less dire poverty ranges
by its side, when the land is not fully pop-
ulated and yet the number of the unem-
ployed reaches to the millions, and all this in

the most prosperous country in the world, with the greatest promise for the future. One is not either an alarmist or a pessimist because he recognizes these facts, and it would be worse than folly to try to blink them out of sight.   I believe that we can deal with them successfully if we will but set ourselves to the grave task, as we have to the trials and dangers of the past.   I am sure that, if these great social problems can be solved anywhere, they can be solved here in the United States.   But the solution will tax to the utmost all the wisdom and courage and learning that the country can provide.   What part are our universities, with their liberal education, to play in the history that is now making and which is still to be written? They are the crown and glory of our civilization, but they can readily be set aside if they fall out of sympathy with the vast movements about them.   I do not say whether they should seek to resist or to sustain, to guide or to control those movements.   But if they would not dry up and wither, they must at least understand them.   A great university must be in touch with the world about it— with its hopes, its passions, its troubles, and its strivings.   If it is not, it must be content

" For aye to be in shady cloister mewed,
  Chanting faint hymns to the cold, fruitless moon."

If it effaces enthusiasm and breeds critics, it
must be content to gather about barren altars
on which the fire has gone out, and to prac-
tise rites from which all meaning has fled.
Such is not the object or purpose of a liberal
education. The university which pretends to
give a liberal education must understand the
movements about it, must see whither the
great forces are tending, and justify its existence by breeding men who by its teachings
are more able than all others to render the
service which humanity is ever seeking. (To
do this a liberal education must first of all
mean that the university which gave it sends
forth men who are fit for life because they
have breathed in the spirit which puts them
in sympathy with their country and their
time.)(They must be men to whom the great
refusal is impossible when their people or
their country call upon them to do their part
either in war or peace.)

THE HOME OF THE CABOTS

THE HOME OF THE CABOTS*

EARLY in May, 1497, a little vessel with some twenty persons on board set sail from Bristol on a voyage of discovery. This year the four hundredth anniversary of that event has been duly commemorated at the place where it occurred. Such occasions have been much the fashion of late on both sides of the Atlantic, owing no doubt to the great advance in historical knowledge and to the increased interest in history which this century has witnessed; but among all the events thus celebrated there is perhaps hardly one which more deserves commemoration than the sailing of the little Bristol vessel four hundred years ago. "We derived our rights in America," said Edmund Burke, "from the discovery of Sebastian Cabot, who first made the Northern Continent in 1497. The fact is sufficiently certain to establish a right to our settlements

* Reprinted from the *Nineteenth Century* (May, 1897), by the kind permission of Mr. James Knowles.

in North America." On that voyage of the Cabots and its results rested the English claim to North America. Under that claim, successfully maintained, Englishmen planted the colonies which reached from Georgia to Maine, and which by their growth finally enabled the mother-country to drive the French from Canada and make the continent from Mexico to the North Pole a possession of the English-speaking race. From those early colonies have come the United States and the Dominion of Canada. The daring voyage of discovery which made these things possible, and gave a continent to the English race, certainly deserves to be freshly remembered.

Burke really stated the whole case in the sentence just quoted, but he made one error. The commander of the ship and the leader of the expedition was not Sebastian but John Cabot. That Sebastian accompanied his father is probable, although not certain; but there is no doubt whatever that John Cabot was the originator, chief, and captain of this famous expedition, so small when it sailed away from Bristol, so big with meaning to mankind when it returned a few months later.

The following year there was another voyage made by the Cabots, with larger results

in the way of exploration and information as
to this new world, which they thought part of
the country of the "Great Cham." Into the
story of these memorable voyages, about
which volumes have been written, or into the
interesting career and long life of Sebastian
Cabot—for John Cabot disappears from our
ken after the second expedition — I do not
propose to enter. My only purpose here is
to try to show who these men were who rendered this great service to England and to
the world, and from what race they sprang.

On this point there have been much expenditure of learning, manifold conjectures, many
theories, and abundant suggestions; but the
upshot of all this labor has been merely one of
those historical puzzles or mysteries in which
the antiquarian mind delights. As a matter of
fact the explanation is very simple, and possibly
that is one reason why it has been overlooked.
By this I do not mean that any one can tell
where John Cabot was born, for no one knows,
nor has any evidence on that point been produced. If some inquirer were to search among
the records of a certain outlying portion of the
United Kingdom, as has not yet been done,
with this object in view, something might be
found which would throw light on John Cabot's

birth and parentage. So far, however, there is no positive evidence whatever in regard to either. The case is hardly better in regard to Sebastian, for when he was trying to leave the service of Spain for that of Venice, he told Contarini that he was born in Venice but brought up in England; while, on the other hand, when he was an old man he told Eden that he was born in Bristol, and carried to Venice by his father at the age of four years. The conflict between Sebastian's own statements is hardly more instructive than the absence of all information in regard to his father. But, although it is impossible to fix the birthplace of either of these men, it is still possible to do that which is perhaps quite as important —determine where the family or the race to which they belonged originated.

John Cabot is always spoken of as a Venetian, and quite properly and correctly, but he was a Venetian by naturalization, not by birth. The first mention of his name in history occurs in the Venetian archives, where we find the record of his admission to citizenship in 1476. Before that there is absolutely nothing, and the Venetian archives simply prove that John Cabot was not born in Venice, and was a Venetian only by adoption. We know that he mar-

ried a Venetian woman, and, from Sebastian's
contradictory statements about his own birthplace, we also know that his father had con-
nections of some sort in England, and passed
much time in that country long before the
famous voyage ; for on that point both Sebastian's versions as to his own nativity agree.
Therefore it was not by accident that John
Cabot went to England, where he had been
in the habit of going, and received from
Henry VII., in 1496, the patent granted to
himself and his three sons, Louis, Sebastian,
and Sanctius, for the discovery of unknown
lands in the eastern, western, or northern seas,
with the right to occupy such territories. The
recent authorities speak of John Cabot as probably born in Genoa or its neighborhood, rest-
ing apparently only on Pedro de Ayala's reference to him as a Genoese and Stowe's loose
statement that Sebastian was " Genoa's son."
All this is mere guesswork. We really know
nothing about John Cabot's birthplace or family, except the not very illuminating fact that
he was not born in Venice.

Let us now turn from the particular to the
general. The Cabots were a numerous race.
We find them scattered all over Europe ; the
name varied a little here and there, but al-

ways easily identified. If it can be shown
that people of that name have a home where
they have lived for many generations, then
the problem of the origin of the Cabot family
is solved. In Ireland and Scotland there have
been septs or clans all bearing a common
name, and, in tradition at least, going back to
a common ancestor. It needs no inquiry to
tell us where the O'Donnells came from, although some of them have been Spaniards for
several generations. We know the origin of
the MacMahons and MacDonalds, of France,
without much research. Wherever one meets
a Cameron or a Campbell, one may be sure
that his genealogy, if duly followed up, will
take us back sooner or later to Scotland. The
same law holds good very often in regard to
families which have no pretence to a tribal
origin or to the dignity of a clan or sept, especially if they come from some island or some
sequestered spot on the main-land.

Such is the case with the Cabots, or Chabots.
The island of Jersey is their place of origin,
and the residence there of men of that name
goes back to a very early period. In Stowe's
list of those who accompanied William the
Conqueror to England we find the name Cabot spelled as it is to-day. The bearer was,

no doubt, one of the many Normans who followed William from the land which their
Norse ancestors had swooped down upon a
century earlier. Whether the particular adventurer who, according to Stowe, came over
with the Conqueror was from the island of
Jersey we have no means of knowing. But
men of that name must have settled in the
island at a very early period, soon after it was
granted as a fief to Rolf the Ganger by Charles
the Simple. Down even to the present time
many of the people in two Jersey parishes
are named Cabot, or Chabot. The word "Chabot" means also a kind of fish and a measure,
and seems to be peculiar in this way to the
island. On the bells of some of the churches,
on the tombstones, and in the *Armorial of
Jersey* the name and arms are also found, and
go back to very early times. The arms, indeed, prove the antiquity of the race in the
island. They are "armes parlantes," three
fishes (chabots), with the pilgrim's scallop shell
for a crest, indicating the period of the Cru-
sades. The motto is one of the ancient pun-
ning mottoes, "Semper cor, caput, Cabot."
These peculiarities of name and arms indicate
the antiquity of the family and also its identi-
fication with that particular spot where the

fish borne upon the shield are indigenous and known by a particular name which gives them appropriateness for the coat-of-arms. The name is also widely diffused in France, where it is found in many noble families, including the Rohans, owing to the *mésalliance*, so criticised by Saint-Simon, of the heiress of the Rohans with Henri de Chabot. In the French dictionaries it is usually stated that the family is ancient and comes from Poitou, where it has been known since 1040, and no doubt many of the name who afterwards reached distinction came from that part of France. The use of the word in common speech for a fish and a measure indicates, however, very strongly that the original seat of the race was on the Channel island of Jersey. The people there were of Norse descent, for the first settlements of the Normans were made along the coast of Normandy. It was, in fact, from that northern coast of France that the Normans spread over England and Europe, going in the course of their wanderings much farther afield than Poitou. But, however this may be, it is clear that the Cabots were of Norman race, and that they settled first on the coast of Normandy with the rest of the adventurers who came down in the wake of Rolf the Ganger. The name has remained unchanged, Cabot, or Chabot, for many centuries. In the letters patent it is spelled exactly as it is to-day — John Cabot. The name is not Italian, nor is it anglicized, but is the Norman-French name, as it has always been known both in the Channel Islands and in Poitou for more than eight hundred years. Tarducci, the latest biographer of the Cabots, in his zeal to prove that they were Italians, produces names from Siena and elsewhere which in sound have a resemblance more or less distant to that of Cabot. But this is labor wasted. The name in Henry's patent was too plain and familiar to have been an anglicized version of some Italian patronymic, and the variations on the names of the discoverers in the various contemporary authorities are merely efforts to make the name Cabot conform to the language of the writer, whether he used Spanish, Italian, or Latin, and nothing more.

There is, however, much better testimony than the name to connect the navigators with the race which multiplied in the Channel island, and which had such numerous representatives in Poitou. In the *Armorial de la Noblesse de Languedoc*, by Louis de la Roque, it is shown that Louis, the son of the navigator, settled at St.-Paul-le-Coste, in the Cévennes, and had a son, Pierre, from whom the family is traced to the present time.   Pierre left a will, in which he stated that he was the grandson of the navigator John.   The decisive point is that the arms of this family are those of the Jersey Cabots precisely — three fishes, motto, and crest, all identical.   Therefore the arms of Louis, the father of Pierre and son of John the navigator, are the Jersey arms, and unite them with the island race.   These same arms, with their fishes, are found among all the French Chabots quartered with those of Rohan and the rest.   They exist unchanged in the American family, which came directly from Jersey to New England in the latter half of the seventeenth century.   The same name and the same arms constitute a proof of identity of race before which the contradictory accounts of contemporaries of the discoverers, void as they are of any affirmative evidence, or the guesses of modern investigators, are of little avail.   The arms also are important in showing, as has been already suggested, that the family started from the island, and not from Poitou; for the chabot was a fish caught in the neighborhood of the islands, a very natural emblem to take there, but not at

all a likely device to have been adopted in
Poitou.

Just where John Cabot was born, as was
said at the outset, no one now can tell, for he
was a wanderer and adventurer like his remote
Norse ancestors, and left no records or papers.
But that he drew his blood from the Norman race of the Channel Islands his name and
arms seem to prove beyond doubt. It is most
probable also that it was not by chance that
he got his patent from an English king, and
sailed on his memorable voyage from an English port. England was not then a sea power,
nor was she numbered among the great trad-
ing and commercial nations of Europe. Venice or Genoa, Portugal or Spain, offered much
larger opportunities and greater encourage-
ment to the merchant or the adventurer than
England. Yet John Cabot came to England
for his letters patent and set out from Bristol
on his voyage of discovery. We know from
Sebastian Cabot's statement that his father
had relations with England, and was much
and often in that country. It is not going
too far to suppose that, when he had made
up his mind to enter upon his voyage of discovery in the New World, he came back to
the land of which the home of his fathers, and

perhaps his own birthplace, was a part. It is certain that no other reason for his doing so is given in any contemporary evidence.

So long as the Cabots performed successfully the great work which it fell to them to do, it perhaps does not matter very much where they were born or whence they came. (Yet there is a satisfaction in knowing that the strongest evidence we have shows that the men who gave England her title to North America, and made it the heritage of the English-speaking people, were of that Norman race which did so much for the making of England, and sprang from those Channel Islands which have been a part of the kingdom of Great Britain ever since William the Conqueror seized the English crown.

ENGLISH ELECTIONS

ENGLISH ELECTIONS

WE have in our Eastern States a few news-papers, with a small number of persons who presumably read those newspapers, which are not only greatly dissatisfied with things American, but which always compare our short-comings with the bright standard of perfection which they tell us exists in England. One of the many subjects of their criticism has been the conduct of our elections, and here, as usual, they are fond of referring us to England, in order to show us by that shining example how far we are from an ideal condition. I happened to be in England in the summer of 1895, while the last general election was in progress, and always having been much interested in all matters relating to the conduct of our own elections, I availed myself of the opportunity thus presented to examine the English methods which have been held up to us by our Anglo-American critics at home as the standard to which we should strive to attain.

The charges usually brought against us by these critics are the violence and disorder of our election contests, the personalities in which we indulge, the campaign stories set afloat to affect votes, and other sharp practices of a like nature: frauds of various kinds in registration and voting, the lavish use of money, and the relentless character of our party discipline. I studied these various points in the English elections which were going on everywhere around me, and tried to make myself familiar with all those features which Anglo-Americans think we should imitate. I intend here to give very briefly the results of my observations.

As to the first point of violence and disorder, I take the following cases as reported in the London *Times*, in order to show the contrast between the quiet and order which prevail in England and the violence and disorder which are said by our critics to characterize our elections. These cases, I admit, present features very different from anything that occurs in American elections. On that point there can be no doubt. Whether we should desire to imitate them is another question, which I will not now discuss.

Here is the first case I find among my clippings from the *Times: "Mr. Disraeli, M.P., Assaulted.*—Mr. Coningsby Disraeli, M.P. for the Altrincham division of Cheshire, was assaulted on leaving the Conservative Club at Altrincham after the close of the poll on Monday. Mr. Disraeli's carriage was surrounded by a disorderly mob, which a force of Cheshire constabulary were unable to keep in check. Stones and bricks were thrown as the carriage drove away, and Mr. Disraeli, besides being struck with a stick, was momentarily stunned by a stone which struck him on the back of the head. The crowd afterwards smashed the windows of the Conservative Club, and a member of the club was struck by a stone and conveyed to the hospital unconscious. The street was ultimately cleared by the police."

Passing from Altrincham to Croydon, we learn that "Excitement is rising in Croydon. Some of Mr. Hutchinson's more violent partisans proceeded to the front of the Central Conservative Club in North End on Saturday and indulged in hooting and yelling, which were kept up until midnight. Several members of the club attempted to address the gathering, but were pelted with eggs and apples for their trouble. Yesterday morning both Mr. Ritchie and Mr. Hutchinson attended divine service at the parish church, and it is stated that the Liberal candidate, while walking down the aisle on his way out at the conclusion of the service, was hissed by a number of ladies, who took up positions on either side of the vestibule."

The next relates to a London division: "*Tower Hamlets* (*St. George's*).—In consequence of the many serious disturbances that have occurred in this division during the progress of the contest, a large number of police were yesterday drafted into the division, with a view of maintaining order. Mr. Marks, who was struck in the eye Tuesday night with a large stone, was yesterday driving about the constituency, accompanied by his wife, with a shade over the injured eye. This unprovoked assault has caused great indignation throughout the division. Several petty disturbances occurred at one or two of the polling-stations, but owing to the presence of the strong force of police nothing serious took place. The excitement became intense as the close of the poll approached, each party exerting itself to the utmost in order to secure the attendance of the electors at the polling booths."

Now comes a case with a touch of humor;

but the polite reply of Mr. Hay to an interruption is a not uninteresting example of English platform manners which we are so often told our campaign speakers ought to copy: "Of the 'dogs of war' most people have heard, but the dog of politics is new. Hitherto that friend of humanity has been remarkable for faithfulness, but he would be a bold man who would answer for him after certain political associations, and his first introduction to public affairs has not been promising. There was a Unionist gathering at Hoxton Church on Saturday, attended by fully two thousand persons, when serious disturbances occurred, owing to a respectably dressed man forcing his way through the crowd with a large mastiff having attached to his collar a card urging the electors to 'Vote for Stuart.' This occasioned a scuffle, ending in a free fight, which the police had to put down. The Hon. Claude Hay, Unionist candidate, then proceeded with his speech, dismissing personal affronts with the declaration that he did not care a button for them, and describing the methods of his interrupters as 'cowardly and un-English.' Pointing to one of the disturbers, he said he could only tell that gentleman he was a liar when he stated that he would not carry out his pledges."

That these disturbances were not mere horse-play the following case at Luton shows plainly: "*Bedfordshire* (*Luton*).—Some rioting took place at Luton on Friday night after the declaration of the poll, and in addition to the reading twice of the Riot Act, the local authorities found it necessary to send for fifty metropolitan police. A local solicitor, who had been previously identified with the Liberal-Unionist party, published on the eve of the poll a pamphlet which the Conservatives considered reflected upon their candidate, Colonel Duke. An angry mob besieged his office, broke his windows, and attempted to gain an entrance. The disturbance continued until one o'clock, when the combined London and local police charged the crowd and dispersed it. At Dunstable, where the solicior in question lives, the mob entered his house and wrecked the furniture."

At Camborne, where Mr. Conybeare was defeated, the contest was heated. A gentleman told me that he happened to meet the election agent of Mr. Strauss, the successful Unionist candidate, and observing that he had a black eye, asked him how he got it. The agent said he was hit at Camborne, and that there were twenty men in

the hospital there as a result of election
fighting.

On August 9th Mr. E. Garnet Man wrote
to the *Times* that he and Mr. Gretton were
"stoned and hustled," and had their meeting
broken up at Church Gresley and Swadlincote
by a mob excited by the harangues of a Non-
conformist minister.

These incidents which I have just cited were
chronicled in the newspapers, but seemed, so
far as I could observe, to pass without comment and quite as matters of course. There
was one case, however, which not only drew
forth a good deal of correspondence, but also
excited some little remark. This was the
East Norfolk election, where Mr. Rider Haggard was the Conservative candidate. He
and his party were mobbed at Ludham and
Stalham. He had ladies with him, and one
of them, Mrs. Hartcup, was seriously injured
by stones which struck her in the head. The
party took refuge from the arguments of their
political opponents in the Swan Hotel at Stalham. There they were besieged by a crowd
for several hours, and were only rescued by
constables armed with cutlasses, who dispersed
the mob. Mr. Haggard wrote with his accustomed force and eloquence to the *Times* about

14

the almost African dangers to which he had been exposed, and the injuries which he and his party had received from the attacks of the mob.   His opponent, Mr. Price, replied, and a long controversy followed.   Among others who took part in it was one who signed herself "A Lady Sufferer," and who seemed disposed to laugh at Mr. Haggard for his complaints, because she too had been stoned when canvassing in the Liberal interests in the same division some years before.   She said, "I took it as part of what I had to bear in the battle of politics," and her letter exhibited a calm philosophy in regard to being made a target for stones and other missiles which, I think, would hardly be shown under like circumstances by American women, even by those anxious to possess the suffrage.

Mr. Haggard's misfortunes were not, however, the only incidents of the East Norfolk election.   In the division of which North Walsam is the political centre a Unionist meeting was held in the market-place.   While it was going on, Lord Wodehouse, the eldest son of the Earl of Kimberly, demanded that Mr. John Gaymer, who presided, should come down from the chair, and on the latter gentleman's displaying some hesitation, "Lord Wodehouse," in the language of the newspaper, "forcibly removed him from the rostrum." Mr. Gaymer returned, by some method not described, to the chair, and then remonstrated with Lord Wodehouse, who continually interrupted him, . and also called out: "Come down and have it out with me. I will fight you for fifty pounds." A few days after, Mr. Gaymer made a complaint against Lord Wodehouse before the magistrates, and the noble lord was fined five pounds for assault. The matter did not, however, end here. Some time after the election was over, the Conservative ministry had Lord Wodehouse removed from the Commission of the Peace, of which he was a member. I think I may go so far as to say, although I have no desire to criticise English election methods, that Lord Wodehouse was guilty of what has been called in this country "offensive partisanship." Yet even here, I think, it would be thought that we were pushing the spoils system pretty far to remove a man from a judicial position on account of his political conduct.

This practice of pelting a candidate and the ladies who accompany him, according to the English custom, is apparently a common diversion in the English elections. Sir William and Lady Harcourt were pelted at Derby, and I saw many allusions to similiar instances. There is no need, however, of multiplying examples. I have given, I think, enough cases to show the orderly methods of political discussion in England which our Anglo-American critics would have us imitate.

In our last Presidential election (1896), which was one of extraordinary excitement and produced great bitterness of feeling, we had some instances of pelting speakers and of shouting them down. In every case the result was a reaction in favor of the persons attacked, and the assaults were denounced by the newspapers without distinction of party. No one defended such performances, still less were they treated as matters of course. The attack with missiles and interruptions upon Mr. Carlisle, at Covington, undoubtedly injured the Democrats and helped the Republicans in Kentucky, while the exploit of the Yale students in howling down Mr. Bryan, at New Haven, was generally condemned and awakened sympathy for the Democratic candidate for the Presidency.

I now come to the matter of charges made against public men during a canvass for the purpose of affecting votes. The London cor-

respondent of the New York *Tribune*, in a letter written at the time, summed up some of
the campaigning in the English elections of
1895 as follows: "Campaign literature by the
ton; roorbacks sprung in Ireland; press ex-
tracts showing how bad an opinion Lord Salisbury once had of Mr. Chamberlain, and how
cordially that dislike was reciprocated by the
Birmingham leader; parallel columns brought
into play against one Unionist leader after another; and criminations about the purchase of
the Ulster votes answered by recriminations
about the government cordite contracts." This
list, however, does not cover by any means all
the charges of a personal character put forward during the canvass.

Mr. Benn, who was running in one of the
London divisions, was attacked by his opponents because his insane brother had in a fit
of madness killed their father. Even in the
politics of "our violent people" a charge of
this sort for political purposes would, I think,
be considered cruel.

But attacks of this kind were not confined
to the lesser candidates. It was freely charged
that Sir H. Naylor-Leyland had changed from
the Conservative to the Liberal side because
the Liberal government had given him a bar-

onetcy.   As to the truth of this charge I have no opinion to express.   I only know that Sir H. Naylor-Leyland was recently made a baronet, and that this pleasant accusation against him and the Liberal government was freely made.

Much more serious, however, was the charge against Lord Rosebery, which played a large part in the campaign, that he had made four peers, in consideration of the gift by these gentlemen of one hundred thousand pounds to the campaign fund of the Liberal party.   Lord Rosebery's secretary, in a letter to the *Times*, said that two of these peerages were conferred upon gentlemen whose merits no one could question, and who were also poor men, and that the other two were given in pursuance of an arrangement made by Mr. Gladstone with which Lord Rosebery had nothing to do.   There were persons who found this answer unsatisfactory, and the matter was much discussed both in the press and on the stump.   This particular charge, moreover, was not made merely by irresponsible orators and newspapers.   Mr. Chamberlain said in a speech at Birmingham, on August 3d: " How can you grant sincerity to a man who in one breath denounces the House of Lords and seeks to

abolish it, and in another gives reason for
the suspicion that he has been selling peerages to the highest bidder." I have no
knowledge whatever as to the foundation of
this charge, but considered merely as a campaign attack on the leader of one of the two
great parties, a man of the very highest character, I think it will be admitted that even the
violence of the American Presidential election
can hardly show anything more serious. In
this connection, however, there is something
more to be said. Since I first noted this
charge and followed its fortunes as it was
tossed back and forth in the excitement of an
election contest, my attention has been called
to some other cases which lead me to believe that the attack on Lord Rosebery and
Mr. Gladstone was not so unusual nor the
charge itself regarded in England as so monstrous as I had supposed. In the *Spectator* for
May 23, 1896, occurs the following statement:
" Lord Salisbury was not distributing them
eccentrically, but according to the regular custom, taking wealthy squires like Mr. E. Hen-
eage and Colonel Malcolm, of Poltalloch, for
his peerages; and giving baronetcies to Mr.
R. U. P. Fitzgerald, Mr. O. Dalgleish, Mr.
Lewis McIver, Mr. J. Verdie, and Mr. C.

Cave, because they are wealthy men who have done service to the party." If this sort of thing is the "regular custom," the charge against Lord Rosebery does not seem very serious material for a party attack, and one cannot see why it was pressed unless the sum supposed to have been paid for those peerages was so large as to be thought exorbitant. If this practice of giving peerages or titles in return for contributions for political purposes is the "regular custom," why is the American habit of appointment to certain public offices outside the classified places for political and party services so monstrous and so painful to our English critics and their followers here? Colonel Higginson, from one of whose delightful essays* I have, in the language of the wise, conveyed this extract from the *Spectator*, pertinently inquires how this system of bartering peerages differs from that of Tammany, except that it is more gilded and veneered. The most that a man gets in the United States is a temporary office with such distinction as it carries and a very modest salary. In England the rich party-worker gets an hereditary dignity, which helps his children,

---

* *Book and Heart.*

at least, to an assured social position; and if a peerage, to a seat in the House of Lords. The money may go, but the peerage and the social position remain. I am not concerned here with the ethics of either method. I merely wish to point out that in principle the system of rewarding political supporters, party-workers, and subscribers on one side of the Atlantic does not differ at all from that in vogue on the other, except that the English give higher prizes and cover the transaction under a name of more lofty sound.

As to the point of illegal practices at registration and elections, I found that they were not unknown in England. In Durham, where the seat was won by one vote, it appeared that the name of a man who was in jail at the time had been voted upon, and it was freely charged that the names of men who were dead were used for the same purpose. This election, I believe, was to be contested. I saw it stated in the *Times* that a man was charged with personation at Birkenhead, and from a single issue of the same newspaper I take the following cases:

At Hartlepool, where the question of presenting a petition against the return of the Unionist candidate was considered, the allegations referred to the distribution of free drinks and other illegal practices.

In the Litchfield division of Staffordshire it was decided to present a petition against the return of Mr. Fulford, and counsel were of the opinion that there was ample evidence of corrupt and illegal practices.

In the Falkirk Burghs a petition was decided upon against the return of Mr. John Wilson, on the ground of alleged bribery by the Unionist agent.

At Wigan, Henry Litherland was summoned before the magistrate for bribing voters.

These cases, as I have said, are taken from a single issue of the *Times*. But under the head of " Ireland," on another day, I find the following statement:

" *Mayo* (*North*).—Our Dublin correspondent, telegraphing last night, says: The defeat of Mr. Egan, the Parnellite candidate, is attributed to clerical intimidation. In a speech to his supporters, after the declaration of the poll, he declared that the intimidation that had been practised plainly showed that there was no liberty of the franchise in North Mayo. Acting under the advice of counsel, he has lodged with the subsheriff an objection against the return of the votes. The validity of more than 400 ballot papers is impugned, and objection is made to blocks of illiterate voters recorded in Belmullet. It is further explained that in certain specific cases the voting was illegally conducted. The people of Ballina do not regard the declared result as at all conclusive, and it is stated that on the disputed votes Mr. Egan would have a small majority. Mr. Egan is determined to fight in the higher courts the gross clerical intimidation practised in Belmullet, Ballycastle, and Crossmolina, the strongholds of Mr. Crilly and Healyism."

These examples merely show that fraudulent practices in elections are known as well in England as in the United States.

I come now to the question of the expenditure of money. This possesses a double interest, because it not only shows us the English practice, but it also throws a great deal of light on the charge so freely made of late years in this country that protection was not only bad economically, but that it led to great corruption, owing to the lavish expenditure in the campaigns of the protected interests. The example of England will enable us to see not only the practice there as to election expenses, but also what the effect of a free-trade system is in keeping down the amount of money expended for campaign purposes.

√The enormous sums spent for election purposes in England at the close of the last century are historic. Fortunes were flung away and great estates crippled, if not ruined, in some of the struggles for a coveted seat, where personal and party passion ran high. It is safe to say that nowhere at any time has money ever been spent with such unbridled profusion for the purpose of influencing votes as in the England of that not very remote period to which I have referred. Even as late as 1867, John Bright said, at Birmingham: " I am not able to say what it has cost to seat those 658 members in that House, but if I said that it has cost them and their friends a million of money (pounds sterling), I should say a long way below the mark. I believe it has cost more to seat those 658 men there than to seat all the other representative and legislative assemblies in the world. There are many members who pay always from £1000 to £15,000 for their election." It is safe to say that there has never been a Presidential election in the United States, not excepting the last, when the total expenses of the two great parties exceeded Mr. Bright's underestimate of a general English election in 1867, and our election of 1896 is the only one that at all equals it.

It is not, however, the election expenses of 1867 that it is proper for us to consider and compare our own with now. We must deal with the England of to-day, where laws have been passed to cure the evils of the use of money at election, so flagrant even thirty years ago.

The corrupt-practices act, which was the result of the movement to purify and reform elections in England, fixes the maximum amount which each candidate can spend in each division of the United Kingdom. The candidates are required by law to make a return of all their expenses, and these returns are published officially. In 1892 the official returns show that there were 670 seats and 1307 candidates. Fifty-six seats were uncontested, and the expenses, therefore, in those cases were little or nothing. The official returns include all the seats, although, of course, if these 56 seats were deducted it would increase the average expenditure for the others. The 1307 candidates in 1892 spent £958,532 (in round numbers, $4,792,660), including the returning officers' charges, and £761,058, or

$3,805,290, exclusive of the returning officers'
charges—that is, for purely political purposes.
The total number of votes polled was 4,605,442,
and the amount of money spent per vote was
four shillings one penny, or just about one
dollar a head. The official returns for 1895
show that there were 670 seats and 1181 candidates. There were, therefore, at least 159
uncontested seats, which, if deducted, would
raise very greatly the average expense of those
contested. Taking them, however, all together
as before, the official report shows that under
the act 1181 candidates spent £773,333, including expenses of returning officers, and excluding expenses of returning officers, £617,996.
This was at the rate of 3s. 8¾d., or about
90 cents, a head, the total number of voters
being 3,867,060. The decline in the number
of voters and in the total expense from 1892
to 1895 was due to the increase in the number
of uncontested seats, for the general interest
was certainly as great in the latter as in the
former year.

It must be remembered, however, that these
are only the official returns of the expenses
allowed to each candidate by the law. The
central committees of the two great parties
and other political committees interested in

special objects of legislation, such as bimetal-
lism or the liquor traffic, spend a great deal of
money for political purposes of which no return is made. I was told by good judges, including leaders of both the great parties, that
the election expenses of one general election
in England, exclusive of returning officers'
charges and of the expenditures by organiza-
tions interested in special subjects, would
reach at least a million pounds. The central
committees, whose funds are very large, furnish, of course, a great deal of the money to
the candidates which appears in the official returns, but they also necessarily spend a good
deal of money which does not appear in the
returns. Nor does the expenditure of money
cease here. I was told, for instance, that in
the Newmarket division, where two very rich
men were running, a great deal of money was
being spent on both sides. I asked how this
could be done under the corrupt-practices act,
and was informed that in this case one of the
candidates gave employment to all the unem-
ployed in the division, thus encouraging many
voters in the support of correct political prin-
ciples, and at the same time relieving the rate-
payers. This may be called a special instance, but it indicates that evasion of the

corrupt-practices act is at least possible. One other fact which I derived from official returns seems to be of more general application. For the week ending July 15th the increase of the revenue from beer (there having been no change in the law) over the same week of the previous year was £337,000, indicating an increased consumption of about one million barrels. The first pollings of the general election took place on July 13th, and continued for about three weeks. The Liberals charged that their opponents were giving free beer to the voters, and this extraordinary rise in the revenue just at election time seems at least to indicate that the consumption of beer increases marvellously in England when voting is to be done.

There is nothing certainly in these facts and figures to indicate that free trade has a depressing or lowering effect on election expenditures. But in making a comparison with our own expenditures I will limit myself to the totals of the official returns for Great Britain, which are very far from representing the amount of money actually spent. According to those returns an election in England costs as nearly as possible from ninety cents to one dollar for every voter. On that basis we were

entitled, if we followed the English example
of moderation in election expenditures, to
have spent in the campaign of 1892 $12,154,-
542, and in that of 1896 at least $15,000,000.
As a matter of fact before 1896 there has
never been a campaign in which the national
committees of the two great American parties
have spent between them three million dollars. Allowing, however, three million to the
two national committees, and two million
more to cover all that is spent in addition outside the two great committees, we have five
million dollars for the expenditures of an
American Presidential election before 1896,
which is at the rate of forty cents per voter,
as against one dollar in England. This is an
excessive estimate, for most of the money of
the national committees is sent to the poorer
States and Congressional districts, in very few
of which, indeed, candidates are to be found
who can afford anything like the average expenditure of an English division. Taking,
then, five million dollars as the expenditure of
the Presidential election, we find that it is
just about the amount actually spent at a
general election in England, and only half
what we should be entitled to spend if we
took the scale of the English official returns

15

per vote as our standard of expenditures.
When, in addition, it is remembered that in
this country we have great distances to cover,
which are unknown in England, and which
add enormously to the expense of campaigning, it will be seen that in the United States,
despite the corrupting influences of protected
industries, we do not spend half the money
which we should spend if we lived up to the
English standard.

If we take the campaign of 1896, the most
expensive we have ever had, although one
party had much more money than the other,
it is safe to say that $6,000,000 would be a
liberal estimate for the expenditures of both
parties, while on the English basis we were entitled to spend $15,000,000. When it is re-
membered, also, that at the close of the campaign the Republican party was spending at
the rate of $25,000 a day for the expenses of
speakers and meetings, had issued and distributed 100,000,000 pamphlets and circulars,
and was publishing matter relating to the campaign in some 15,000 newspapers, it is easy
to see that there could not have been much
money left for the purchase of votes. One
rather wonders indeed what becomes of a
nearly equal amount spent in England, where

distances are short, where the campaign lasts
three weeks instead of four months, and where
the number of votes polled is only about one
quarter as many as were thrown in the United
States in 1896. These facts and comparisons,
which I offer without comment, are, I think,
worthy of consideration by those who think
we can escape from the use of money at elections by purifying our system after the English
fashion and adapting ourselves to the English
model. Perhaps we should improve morally if
we did so, but we should certainly spend from
twice to three times as much money as we do
now at a Presidential election, which seems,
whatever else may be said of it, a queer kind
of cure for any political evil.

As to party discipline and party feeling, it
seemed to me that they were much the same
in England as in the United States. The
great body of voters there, as here, remain
firm in their party allegiance. Between them
is the shifting vote which cannot be depended
on, and which usually determines the fate of
elections, except in a case of a great party revolt. In all the political talk which I heard,
and at the time I was in England everybody
was talking politics, I should say that there
was an even keener partisanship shown than

in this country. In Parliament party discipline is much stronger than with us, although,
as I have said, there is no perceptible difference in the discipline of the great body of
voters. The cause of this severer discipline in
Parliament lies, of course, in the English system of government. The ministry is a committee of both Houses. They have a power
to dissolve at any moment, and they therefore
hold over all their followers the great control
which comes from the ability to turn them out
of office and force them to the expense of an
election, and possibly to the loss of their seats.
Under these circumstances it is no wonder
that party discipline in Parliament is so very
strong.

In writing thus of some of the facts in regard to the English elections, I have not had
the slightest intention of criticising their methods or finding fault with them. They are not
perfect ; they have their defects, like our own ;
but also, like our own, I have no doubt whatever that English elections in the main are
fair and free, and that they express, as ours
do, the honest will of the voters. I took occasion to go over to the Battersea division, in
London, where John Burns was running, in
order to see the polling. The officers in charge

of the polling-booth which I visited very kindly admitted me behind the rail, so that I could
see the voting in progress. The system is exactly the same as that of my own State. It
is the secret, or Australian, ballot, and proceeds
much more rapidly than with us, because they
vote only for one, or at the most two or three
candidates. All the proceedings were quiet and
orderly. There was a small crowd outside the
polling-place who chaffed the voters good-
naturedly as they went in, but there was not
the slightest sign of disorder of any kind. I
also visited some polling-places in the adjoin-
ing Clapham division. Here the voting was
proceeding even more quickly and quietly, if
possible, than in Battersea.

My purpose in what I have said here of
English elections, and in the analysis which I
have given of their election expenditures, has
been merely to show that they do not differ
materially from ours, although money is so
much more freely used in England than with
us. The moral to be drawn from it all is that
we should seek by every means in our power
to remedy any evils in our own system and to
guard against all dangers to the ballot-box.
But this can best be done by attending to our
own affairs, guided by general standards of

what is wise and right, and not by nervously and weakly seeking to imitate other people. There is no perfection to be found in English election methods. They have their problems as we have ours. We can manage our own troubles best in our own way, and despite the outcries of the Anglo-Americans in some of our larger cities, it may be safely said that English election methods are very much like those of English-speaking people elsewhere, and that human nature is not materially different in England from that in the United States, so far, at least, as election contests are concerned.

OUR FOREIGN POLICY

OUR FOREIGN POLICY

DURING the last four years questions of our relations with other countries, and involving our interests outside our own borders, have filled a large place in our politics, awakened public attention, and aroused discussion both in Congress and the press. One of these questions has been settled; the others are still with us. Their presence, meaning, and importance alike merit serious study, and cannot be intelligently disposed of by epithets or sneers. Why is it that our foreign policy and our foreign relations have thus come within a comparatively short period so strongly and irrepressibly to the front? The fact is of itself momentous enough, the issues involved sufficiently grave, to deserve a calmer consideration and a more candid discussion than are always accorded to them.

Those who are opposed to our having any foreign policy at all, and who desire to repress these questions of foreign relations altogether, have various explanations to account for their appearance, which are easily stated, because they required but slight labor in invention or construction. One or two able editors, for example, who have abandoned the country of their birth without acquiring any other, and are therefore as well able to judge of patriotism as a blind man of a picture, set down the whole thing as an outburst of pseudo-patriotism. Another equally thoughtful solution is that those Americans who advocate a distinct foreign policy for the United States are simply demagogues, playing to the galleries and seeking applause from that source; and it is asserted that the questions of our foreign relations have been created in this way. If this view is correct, there is certainly no reason for anxiety on the part of those who suggest it; for playing to the galleries, while it may give a momentary triumph to the performer, rarely leads to any serious results either on the stage or in real life. Again, those who cater for the English market explain the phenomena by saying that the whole business is an appeal to the Irish vote. This is, no doubt, satisfying to the London editorial mind, but, as a theory, it seems to lack breadth, for many of the questions which have involved our foreign relations do not concern England at all. Still another explanation is that it is all a matter of party politics. This sounds pleasant and satisfactory, but it is a little obscure, as on all the foreign questions which have arisen party lines have been entirely broken.

All these explanations, and there are others of a similar character which I have not enumerated, however they differ, agree on one point—that these foreign questions have been artificially forced forward, that they are the work of a few newspapers and of a few violent and unscrupulous public men, chiefly in the Senate, and that those who support a strong foreign policy are in every instance advocating something new and unheard of in American politics. If this be true, then the public men and editors, whom their opponents, with singular poverty of invention but with admirable fidelity to British precedents, call "jingoes," are not merely dangerous and unscrupulous, but they are persons of extraordinary power, for they have performed the unexampled feat of creating from nothing not one but a series of great and far-reaching political questions. Unfortunately for this theory, such an exploit is quite impossible. Great political questions, whether foreign or domestic, cannot be created from nothing by any man or by any set of men. They spring from existing conditions; they come from the social, economic, or political development of mankind; they usually have their roots deep down in a distant past, and all men can do is to point them out, call attention to them, take sides about them, fight over them, and in some fashion or other settle them.

The questions of foreign policy which have been so prominent in the United States during the last four years are simply products of this same general law. If we look at them carefully we can readily discover why they are here and what are the reasons of their existence. The first cause is of world-wide scope. (Economic conditions into which it is needless to enter, but which of late have exerted a constantly increasing pressure both upon governments and people, have been forcing nations and individuals alike in the Old World to seek everywhere for fresh outlets for population and new opportunities for commerce, trade, and money-making, In the fierce rivalry thus engendered, the great powers of Europe have reached out in all directions and seized the waste places of the earth. With especial rapacity they have grasped for every bit of land where there was a chance of finding gold. In this way, and with these incentives, Africa has been parcelled out among the great powers of Europe. England has won a number of glorious victories over negro tribes; France has seized on Madagascar; Italy has been badly beaten in Abyssinia; even Germany has taken a share in the Dark Continent. In the far East it is the same story. England and France have been dividing Siam, while Russia is coming down with her railroad to the Pacific, taking a large slice of China on the way.

So long as this process of seizing land was confined to Asia and Africa it did not concern the people of the United States, except as an interesting exhibition of the march of civilization. But a movement of this kind driven by great forces does not stop of its own accord at any given point. The same policy which had been adopted in Africa was applied to the islands of the Pacific. In a few years these were all absorbed by European powers, but chiefly by England. Nothing practically escaped except the Samoan group and the Sandwich Islands. The former were saved by the intervention of the United States, which resulted in the Berlin agreement. The importance to the United States, both on mili-

tary and commercial grounds, of a foothold in
the South Pacific is, one would suppose, sufficiently obvious, yet the last administration
did its best to withdraw from the Berlin agreement, abandon our influence and control in
the Samoan group, and give up our valuable
right to the harbor of Pago - Pago. Luckily
this attempt to withdraw failed, and we still
retain our interest in Samoa.

Far more important than Samoa are the
Sandwich Islands, and there the pressure of
the movement from Europe began to be felt
after the seizure of the rest of the Pacific
islands was completed. In this connection it
will be well to show that the European movement for the seizure of land everywhere is not
a figure of speech, and at the same time to
demonstrate how real and great was the im-
pulse which forced Samoa and Hawaii forward
as living questions in American politics. In
1888 Great Britain took the Gilbert group of
twelve islands, 1500 miles from Hawaii; the
Ellice group of five islands, 1800 miles from
Hawaii; the Enderbury group of five islands,
1600 miles from Hawaii; the Union group
of three islands, 1800 miles from Hawaii;
and Kingman, Fanning, Washington, Palmyra,
Christmas, and Jarvis islands. She also took,

still in the same year, Malden, Starbuck, Du-
dosa, Penrhyn, Vostok, Flint, and Caroline
islands. In 1889 she took Ruic Island, 2400
miles from Hawaii; Suwaroff Island, 1900
miles from Hawaii, and the Coral Islands, 900
miles from Hawaii. In 1891 she took Johnston Island, 600 miles from Hawaii; in 1892,
Gardner Island, 1600 miles from Hawaii; and
in the same year Danger Island, 1800 miles
from Hawaii. The islands of Palmyra and
Johnston had been in possession of the Hawaiian government since 1854, and are still
claimed as a part of Hawaiian territory.

This record, including the seizure of two
islands claimed by Hawaii, a very weak power,
seemed to indicate that England meant to ab-
sorb every Pacific island she could reach, and
that she might be persuaded to take the Sandwich Islands if they came in her way. It was
all done silently and efficiently by the law of
the strongest, and it was this advance which
brought the European movement into contact
with American interests. We had nothing to
do with it. The aggression was not ours.

With Hawaii, therefore, came the first of
those questions of foreign policy which have
disturbed so much those persons in the United
States who are either colonial or cosmopolitan

in their predilections. In that connection for
the first time was heard the outcry about
"jingoism," and the declaration that an attempt was being made to drag the United
States into new and untried paths, and to un-
settle the established order of things in order
to do so.

Let us see just how new the subject was.
So far as those islands of the Hawaiian group
were concerned, the work of introducing Western civilization had been done by Americans.
American influence had always been para-
mount there, and an American settlement or
colony had been long established. Politically
our relations with Hawaii have always been
close and of an exceptional character. Those
relations cannot be more tersely and accu-
rately described than in the words of Senator
Davis, in the very able speech which he made
on this subject in 1894:

"For more than fifty years, as a matter of
announced national policy on the part of this
government, acquiesced in by Hawaii and by
the nations of the civilized world, those islands
have been entailed to the United States, and
as to the United States have been in reversion
when the time should come when the fleeting
monarchy which has existed there should

expire. There has not been a Secretary of State since 1840 who has not announced this determination and this policy. Mr. Webster, Mr. Legaré, Mr. Marcy, Mr. Buchanan, Mr. Seward, Mr. Blaine, and all who have held that office have spoken in the voice of their government in this respect with no uncertain tone, and it has been acquiesced in by foreign nations. So that it is neither extraordinary nor remarkable that at some time, under favorable circumstances and conditions, that to which manifest destiny had dedicated those islands should be brought to pass. Indeed, in 1854, Mr. Marcy, then being Secretary of State, a treaty of annexation was negotiated, and only failed of confirmation because of its condition respecting pecuniary compensation to be made, and because of the fact that the treaty provided that the islands of Hawaii should become a State in the Union."

So it appears, when we leave the region of outcries and come to that of historical facts, that Hawaii has been the peculiar care of this nation for half a century, and that the military and commercial importance of the islands and the welfare of the American colony there have been fully understood by successive administrations of all parties. Those who took up

16

and supported Hawaiian interests in Congress,
therefore, were the conservative followers of
the traditional policy of the United States,
and those who opposed them were the innovators. Even after the Hawaiian treaty of
annexation was withdrawn by Mr. Cleveland,
the Senate without a dissenting voice passed
a resolution declaring that the attempt of any
other nation to take possession of the Sandwich Islands would be regarded as an act of
hostility by the United States. Since then a
new danger has arisen from the Japanese, who
are seeking to get control of the islands by
pouring in colonists, and the United States
must now determine whether they will control
and protect the islands or shrink from the
responsibility and allow the islands to seek
safety under the British flag; for we can no
longer refuse either to act ourselves or to
allow any one else to act. President McKinley
has met and practically settled the question
by sending to the Senate a new treaty of annexation by which, or by resolution, the islands
will be joined to the United States. The military and commercial reasons for this step are
conclusive. Even more conclusive are the ob-
ligations to the people of the island which tradition and good faith alike impose upon us.

The small and select band who judge our foreign policy by the criticism of the wishes of England will be disturbed. There is also the pitiful objection that taking the islands may raise some problems and cause us a little expense and trouble, as if the people who have conquered a continent and fought the greatest war of modern times could not manage a little group of Pacific islands. But this is not the place to discuss the merits or to defend our policy in regard to Hawaii. All I desire to show here is that the question was forced forward by the European movement for the seizure of all land everywhere not held by a strong hand, and that the party which urged action on the part of the United States was pursuing the established policy of fifty years, while their opponents were the advocates of a wholly new policy in this direction, and one which was not entitled historically to be called American.

Such was the foreign question which arose in the West gravely affecting our future in the Pacific, where our commercial extension and development must largely be. But the same forces which operated there were at work elsewhere, and were threatening us in a far more vital point. The land-hunger which had led to the partition of Africa was not likely to be satisfied while anything else remained undevoured. South America, with many weak governments, and with almost endless quantities of rich and unoccupied land, was, and is still, very tempting. England already had a foothold there, and under the new pressure a difficulty which had been dragging along for many years suddenly became acute. The unsettled boundary between British Guiana and Venezuela, which had been moving to the westward for some time, began to jump forward with leaps and bounds, stimulated by the discovery of gold-mines, and by the natural desire on the part of Great Britain to control the Orinoco, one of the great river systems of the continent. For twenty years we had been trying through the ordinary diplomatic channels, and by courteous representations, to induce Great Britain to settle the boundary question with Venezuela by arbitration. All our efforts had been in vain, but by the year 1895 it had become apparent that unless we were prepared to see South America share sooner or later the fate of Africa it was necessary for us to intervene. If Great Britain was to be permitted to take the territory of Venezuela under pretext of a boundary dispute, there was nothing to prevent her taking the whole of Venezuela or any other South American state. If Great Britain could do this with impunity, France and Germany would do it also. These powers, as has been pointed out, had already seized the islands of the Pacific and parcelled out Africa. If the United States were prepared to see South America pass gradually into the hands of Great Britain and other European powers, and to be hemmed in by British naval posts and European dependencies, there was, of course, nothing more to be said. But this onward movement of Great Britain came in conflict with the Monroe Doctrine, which the United States has ever sustained at all hazards. This doctrine was therefore at once invoked by Mr. Olney, who saw clearly the meaning of the Venezuelan question, and who possessed the power and the ability to deal with it.

A great deal of discussion, both then and since, has been devoted to the Monroe Doctrine, but in reality it is not in the least complicated. It is merely the corollary of Washington's neutrality policy, which declared that the United States would not meddle with, or take part in, the affairs of Europe. The Monroe Doctrine announced it to be the settled policy of the United States to regard any attempt on the part of any European power to conquer an American state, to seize territory other than that which they then held, or to make any new establishment in either North or South America, as an act of hostility towards the United States, and one not to be permitted.   In other words, the Monroe Doctrine forbids any territorial aggression or extension, whether permanent or nominally temporary, on the American continents by any European power.   It was at once said, when this question arose, that the Monroe Doctrine was not a principle of international law, and had never been enforced.   It is certainly not a principle of international law any more than the independence of the American colonies, when it was first asserted, was a principle of international law.   We declared and established that independence and secured for it the recognition of the civilized world.   Other nations continue to recognize it, not because it is a principle of international law, but because it is a fact with which it is not wholesome to quarrel.   Moreover, the Monroe Doctrine rests on the great principle of self-preservation, which is much older than international law, and is recognized by it.   Any nation has the right to interfere in regard to another

country if its own safety is involved, and the
Monroe Doctrine is merely the application of
this principle limited in its scope to the American hemisphere.

As to the second point made at that time—
that the doctrine had not been enforced—the
case is equally clear. The Monroe Doctrine
has been observed since its declaration by
other nations out of deference to the United
States. But one instance has arisen, prior to
the Venezuelan case, in which an infraction
was forcibly and seriously attempted, and then
the doctrine was vigorously vindicated. The
Emperor of the French undertook to establish an empire with a European emperor in
Mexico. We were hampered at the moment
by a great civil war, but the despatch from
Mr. Seward, which carried to our representatives abroad the news of Lee's surrender, bore
also instructions to our Minister in France to
notify the French government, in diplomatic
language, that if the French armies were not
withdrawn from Mexico we would march five
hundred thousand men down there if necessary
and put them out. General Sheridan, with a
strong army, was immediately ordered to the
Mexican boundary, and the only mistake made
was in not allowing him to immediately cross

the frontier and expell the French.   Mr. Seward, however, preferred the slower methods
of diplomacy, and in the course of two years
attained his object completely.   The French
abandoned Mexico, and Maximilian was left
to his fate.   There can be little question that
at the time both the French government and
the luckless Maximilian were quite aware that
the Monroe Doctrine was a vital principle, and
that it was dangerous to infringe upon it.

✓ There can be no doubt that the effort of
England to extend her South American possessions under pretext of a boundary dispute
was an infraction of the doctrine as originally
declared.   But whether it was or not, we had
the right to intervene, because we believed
our own safety was threatened by the incep-
tion of a policy which would have led, in its
expansion, to the partition of South America,
and to the establishment in this hemisphere
of powerful neighbors, whose presence would
have compelled us to become a great military
power, and at the same time would have en-
dangered the existence of our trade and commerce with the South American states.

We were wise enough to take to heart the
words of Junius: "One precedent creates another.   They soon accumulate and constitute

law. What yesterday was fact to-day is doctrine." We acted on the sound principle of
obsta principiis. Mr. Olney sent a strong note
in July, 1895. Lord Salisbury replied, not
only controverting our position as to Venezuela, but attacking the validity of the Monroe Doctrine itself. Then, in December, Mr.
Cleveland sent his famous message. England
was surprised, in part with reason and in part
without. She was surprised, with reason, because the American Ambassador and the
American correspondents of the London newspapers at that time had misled her as to
American feeling and intentions. She was
surprised, without reason, because she had
wilfully misconstrued our courteous remon-
strances for twenty years back on this subject.
Englishmen are prone to mistake civility
for servility. The words sound somewhat
alike, but there is really a great difference between them, and it was just here that England
made her error. Complaint was made at the
time, both in England and among her supporters here, that Mr. Cleveland's message,
especially the last clause, was rough and un-
diplomatic. It was rough; but mildness had
failed and roughness succeeded. Where polite and earnest remonstrance had proved

wholly ineffective, a little plain speech was entirely successful.   Thackeray says somewhere: "If a man's foot is in your way and he will not remove it, stamp on it.   He will not like you, but he will take his foot out of the way." It is very unpleasant to do such things, but sometimes it becomes absolutely necessary. Mr. Cleveland was rough; Congress and people came to his support, and we have settled the Venezuelan question.   The Monroe Doctrine has been vindicated, and South America will not be treated like Africa.   In the general popular approval which followed Mr. Cleveland's action, the opponents of any vigorous policy anywhere were silenced for the moment.   But it was only for a moment.   Stocks had declined, and the cry of "jingo," and "war," and "dangerous and revolutionary policy" broke out strongly.   Yet the President and Congress and the American people had merely been true to what had been the traditional policy of the country for more than seventy years.   Those who opposed them were the innovators in American politics.   A weak yielding in the case of Venezuela meant the repetition of similar attempts, and the further seizure of territory in the Americas, and that would have brought war, and probably many

wars, in its train. The determined and successful resistance of the United States at the start
meant peace and the avoidance of a fruitful
cause of war. The President and Congress
were aiding the cause of lasting peace for the
United States. Those who opposed them
were doing what little they could to make us
a military power, and bring on war. Nothing
for more than fifty years at least has done so
much for our permanent peace and welfare as
the stand we took in regard to Venezuela.
Nothing of late years certainly has done so
much to improve our relations with England
as our attitude on this question, for England
has respect only for the strong, bold, and successful. She now understands our position in
regard to the Monroe Doctrine. She misun-
derstood it before, and misapprehension breeds
differences while understanding and knowledge
tend to friendship.

Both Venezuela and Hawaii were forced
upon us by the new movement emanating
from Europe, which has developed within a
recent and comparatively short period. The
Cuban question came in a somewhat different
way, but equally without instigation or suggestion from the United States. There can
be no doubt that the same economic condi-

tions which underlie the European seizure of land in all parts of the world also affected Cuba. The general decline in the world's prices, the increasing pressure of existing debts, and the heightened severity of competition, which set the powers of Europe in motion to seize, divide, and occupy all parts of the earth on which they could lay their hands, fostered and stimulated the conditions which have led to the present revolt in Cuba. But behind these recent influences lies one much older and far more efficient—the determination of the Cubans to free themselves from the corruption and oppression of Spanish government, undoubtedly the most intolerable now borne by any Western people, except those who are so unhappy as to form a part of the Turkish dominions. In Cuba, therefore, the troubles are primarily political, and are of long standing.

When the other Spanish-American colonies revolted from the mother-country, Cuba remained faithful, and no revolution broke out in the island. The success, however, of the continental colonies in establishing their independence gradually made itself felt. In 1825 Bolivar offered to invade the island, where numerous societies were formed to support him ; but the invasion was checked by the intervention of our government, which advised against it. Spain acted after her kind. Instead of ignoring the evidences of sympathy which had been shown towards Bolivar's proposed invasion, the Spanish government, by an ordinance of the 28th of May, gave the captain-general all the powers granted to the governors of besieged towns—that is to say, it put the whole island under martial law. With this piece of needless and sweeping tyranny resistance to Spain began in Cuba and has continued at shortening intervals to the present day, each successive outbreak becoming more formidable and more desperate than the one which preceded it.

In 1826 an insurrection broke out, and its two chiefs were executed. Soon after came another, known as the " Conspiracy of the Black Eagle," which was also repressed, and those engaged in it were imprisoned, banished, or executed. In 1837 the representatives of Cuba and Porto Rico were excluded from the Cortes on the ground that the colonies were to be governed by special law. In 1850 and 1851 occurred an expedition for the liberation of Cuba, and the death of its leader, Narcisso Lopez. There

were also expeditions under General Quitman
and others, and in 1855 Ramon Pinto was put
to death and many other patriots banished.
After this, for a number of years, the Cubans
attempted by peaceful methods to secure from
the government at Madrid some relief from
the oppression which weighed upon them, and
some redress for their many wrongs. All their
efforts came to naught, and such changes as
were made were for the worse rather than for
the better.

The result of all this was that in 1868 a revolution broke out under the leadership of Ces-
pedes. The revolutionists did not succeed in
getting beyond the eastern part of the island,
but they were successful in many engagements.
They crippled still further the already broken
power of Spain, and they could not be put
down by force of arms. The war dragged on
for ten years, and was brought to an end only
by a treaty in which Martinez Campos, in the
name of Spain, promised to the Cubans certain
reforms, to secure which they had taken up
arms. In consideration of these reforms the
insurgents were to abandon their fight for independence, lay down their arms, and receive
a complete amnesty. The insurgents kept
their word. They laid down their arms and

abandoned their struggle for independence. Spain unhesitatingly violated the agreement. With a cynical disregard of good faith, her promise of amnesty was only partially kept, and she imprisoned or executed many who had been engaged in the insurgent cause, while the promised reforms were either totally neglected or carried out by some mockery which had neither reality nor value.* The result of this treachery, of the bloodshed which accompanied it, and of the increased abuses in government which followed, was that the Cubans began again to prepare for revolt, and in February, 1895, the present revolution broke out. The struggle now going on has developed much more rapidly than any which preceded it, and has been marked by far greater successes than the Cubans were able to obtain in the war which lasted from 1868 to 1878. In the preceding rebellion, which was maintained for ten years, the insurgents never succeeded in getting beyond the great central province of Santa Clara, and

* See pamphlet by Adam Badeau, Consul-General in Cuba, 1885; also statement of General Tomaso Estrada Palma, printed for use of Senate Committee on Foreign Relations, 1896; and article by Clarence King in *The Forum* for September, 1895.

their operations were practically confined to the mountainous region in the eastern end of the island. They now control all the island except the cities garrisoned by the Spanish. It is not my purpose, however, to enter into any discussion of the details of the present war. It is enough to show that for seventy years rebellions have broken out in Cuba at short intervals, each one being worse than its predecessor, and proving plainly that Spanish rule and peace are an impossible combination in the island.

The next point is as to our own policy in the past in regard to Cuba. The many civil wars in Cuba have given abundant opportunity for declarations of that policy and for learning what the action of our government has been. John Quincy Adams, when Secretary of State, instructed our minister to Spain as follows:

"These islands [Cuba and Porto Rico] from their local position are natural appendages to the North American continent, and one of them, Cuba, almost in sight of our shores, has, from a multitude of considerations, become an object of transcendent importance to the commercial and political interests of our Union. . . . Such indeed are, between the interests of that island and this country, the geographical, commercial, moral, and political relations formed by nature, gathering in the process of time, and even now verging to maturity, that in looking forward to the probable course of events for the short period of half a century, it is scarcely possible to resist the conviction that the annexation of Cuba to our federal republic will be indispensable to the continuance and integrity of the Union itself. . . . Cuba, forcibly disjointed from its own unnatural connection with Spain, and incapable of self-support, can gravitate only towards the North American Union, which by the same law of nature cannot cast her off from its bosom."

Henry Clay, the successor of Adams in the Department of State, wrote as follows, likewise to our minister at the Spanish Court:

" If the war should continue between Spain and the new republics, and those islands [Cuba and Porto Rico] should become the object and theatre of it, their fortunes have such a connection with the prosperity of the United States that they could not be indifferent spectators, and the possible contingencies of such a protracted war might bring upon the government of the United States duties and obliga-

17

tions, the performance of which, however painful it should be, they might not be at liberty to decline."

At a later day Edward Everett declared that the Cuban question was an American question, and must be so regarded by other nations. We have formally declared that we should not permit the transfer of Cuba to any other European power, and have always and uniformly assumed that the fate of that island, lying as it does at our very doors, was of vital importance to the United States. By this declaration we have not only shut out all European powers except Spain from the island, but we have incurred a responsibility towards the Cubans which we can neither disguise nor escape.

During the last Cuban war we adhered firmly to our traditional attitude, and did not hesitate to take steps looking towards the separation of the island from the government of Spain.

This was the policy pursued by Mr. Fish, who endeavored to purchase Cuban independence from Spain. It was approved at that time by Mr. Sumner, although he felt a very natural reluctance to extend any help to the Cubans while negro slavery still existed in the island. At a later date, in 1876, Mr. Fish declared that the United States would intervene unless the war was brought to an end—a declaration that undoubtedly hastened the concessions which stopped hostilities.

We can learn the views of American statesmen at that time from the words of Sumner, in 1869:

" For myself I cannot doubt that in the interest of both parties, Cuba and Spain, and in the interest of humanity also, the contest should be closed. This is my judgment on the facts, so far as known to me. Cuba must be saved from its bloody delirium, or little will be left for the final conqueror. Nor can the enlightened mind fail to see that the Spanish power on this island is an anachronism. The day of European colonies has passed—at least in this hemisphere, where the rights of man were first proclaimed and self-government first organized."

It would not be easy to improve on Mr. Sumner's statement of the larger aspects of the Cuban question, and in making it he merely followed the line marked out by Clay and Adams and Everett. There is nothing new, therefore, in the position of those who believe that the Cuban question is one of supreme importance to the United States, with which we

are immediately concerned, and which it be-
hooves us in the interests of humanity, of business, and political prudence alike to bring to
a final settlement. The new ground is that
taken by those Americans who oppose Cuba
and the Cubans and take the side of Spain.

It is worth while to consider for a moment
what is said for this new position in our politics and foreign policy. One objection to the
Cuban cause is that the Cubans are of different race and creed, of Spanish extraction, and
with many people of mixed blood among them.
As to the validity of this objection I will say
nothing, for I desire to enumerate objections
rather than try to confute them. Yet it may
be observed in passing that this particular
proposition is both queer and novel among a
people who asserted that all men were created equal, and who have also the distinguished
honor to be the countrymen of Abraham
Lincoln.

Another objection, always brought forward
as conclusive, is that those who sympathize
with Cuba and with a prompt settlement of
the Cuban question desire war. This is mere
outcry and an appeal to fear and greed. A
firm attitude is the best promoter of peace.
Weakness and vacillation are the surest in-

centives to war. It is, for instance, part of
what is called the "jingo" policy to desire
the purchase of the Danish Islands. It was
the policy of Lincoln and Seward to obtain
these islands for a naval station, and here again
the "jingo" of to-day is in accord with the
opinion and the action of the greatest statesmen of the past. But there is more in this
than the acquisition of a naval station. Den-
mark desires to part with these islands. She
would like to sell them to us, but there are
other possible purchasers. The German Emperor is said to covet them. An attempt on
the part of Germany to take them would lead
to serious trouble, if not to war, with the
United States. Our purchase of the islands,
on the other hand, would at once remove all
possibility of trouble with any other nation
over their possession, and would therefore be
preeminently a peace measure.

The case of the Danish Islands illustrates
on a small scale the true course in the much
larger and graver question of Cuba. That the
condition of the island is an anxiety and an-
noyance, that American property is destroyed,
that the war causes alarm to business, are all
due to the simple fact that Cuba belongs to
Spain. So long as that ownership continues,

anxiety, agitations, and alarms of war are sure
to continue also, in connection with it. Thus
we come to the great principle which under-
lies nearly every phase of our foreign policy.
In 1776 we ourselves began the movement to
drive Europe out of America. We succeeded
in our effort. The people of South America
followed our example and expelled the government of Spain. In these days, when it is
the fashion to sneer at the Cubans, it may not
be amiss to recall the fact that Bolivar was
looked upon in the United States as a hero
and called a second Washington. The Monroe Doctrine, which followed, was but a declaration to the same effect that European governments must not return to the places from
which they had been expelled, nor seek to ac-
quire new territory in the Americas. The re-
peated revolts in Cuba result from the operation of the same forces. It is part of the
movement which we began more than a hundred years ago, and the historical and political evolution which it represents may be
delayed, but cannot be stopped. As Sumner
said, European colonial government is an anachronism in this century in the Americas.
Ever since we started the movement ourselves
we have fostered and sympathized with it,

and this course has been not only natural, but right. Practically all our difficulties with other nations, except under the abnormal conditions of our civil war, have been due solely to the possession of colonies in this hemisphere by European powers. Aside from the Mexican war, we have never been disturbed by our neighbors to the south, and have easily settled our occasional disagreements with them. But where European possessions exist, there our serious troubles outside our own borders have arisen. One strong reason for the regard felt for Russia in the United States is that she recognized these conditions in the Western hemisphere, voluntarily withdrew from America, and sold us Alaska. On the other hand, all our troubles with England have grown out of her rule in Canada, and if it were not for Canada it would be difficult to conceive of anything which could disturb our relations with Great Britain. The same is true in even greater degree of Spain, whose colonial government is oppressive and corrupt. We do not seek or desire the annexation of Cuba, but it is for the highest interests and for the peace of the United States, to say nothing of the large gain to humanity and civilization, that Spain should be driven out and the island be-

come an independent republic. Those who
desire a firm and positive attitude in regard to
Cuba not only sustain the true and traditional
policy of the United States, but also follow
the course of action which makes most surely
for our own peace and welfare. Those who
oppose such a policy are in this as in other instances the innovators. They keep alive a dangerous situation, and they set themselves to
resist the whole course of the social and political evolution of the last hundred years on the
American continents.

Moreover, behind all these political, historical, and economical reasons for standing by
the traditional foreign policy of the United
States lies the natural sentiment of the American people. We sympathize instinctively with
the movement to drive European rule from
the Americas, and with men who are struggling
anywhere for freedom and for the right to govern themselves. In certain quarters to-day it is
the fashion to sneer at this American sentiment and to ask why we should sympathize
with the Cubans or waste thought upon them.
As it is a matter of sentiment, and as right
sentiment has and ought to have a large part
in the affairs of men, perhaps we cannot answer the inquiry of this new school of Ameri-

cans better than by Browning's noble lines to
some one who asked him why he was a
Liberal :

" But little do or can the best of us;
   That little is achieved through Liberty.
Who then dares hold—emancipated thus—
   His fellow shall continue bound ? Not I
Who live, love, labor freely, nor discuss
   A brother's right to freedom—That is 'why.'"

This has ever been the sentiment of America. When the modern friends of Spain in the
United States jeeringly ask why we should
trouble ourselves about the Cubans or Arme-
nians or Cretans, and go so far afield with our
sympathies, they fail to remember the history
of their own country. They forget the Congress which, stirred by the splendor of Webster's eloquence, sent words of encourage-
ment to the Greeks. They forget whose sympathies went far across the waters to the
Hungarians, and who were the people who
brought Kossuth to safety in one of their own
men-of-war, while through the lips of Webster they rebuked the insolence of Austria.
Sympathy for men fighting for freedom anywhere is distinctively American, and when
from fear or greed or from absorption in mere-

ly material things we despise and abandon it,
we shall not only deny our history and our
birthright, but our faith in our own Republic,
and all we most cherish will fade and grow dim.

This opposition to the popular and public
sympathy for those who seek freedom and resist oppression finds expression also in other
ways. It leads some of its adherents from
hostility to the Cubans to opposition to building and maintaining a proper navy and to
the construction of coast defences. Here it is
again in flagrant contradiction to the policy
which Washington declared, and to which we
have always tried to be true, that in time of
peace we should be prepared for war, because
in that way alone could peace be preserved.
We paid heavily in the war of 1812 for the
abandonment of Washington's policy by Jefferson, and we learned our lesson not only
from our sufferings in that war, but from the
victories of our ships on lake and ocean.
From that time until the civil war it was our
consistent policy to maintain a navy of mod-
erate size but of the highest efficiency, and
composed of ships of the best type in each
class. On the same theory, and taught by the
same experience, we fortified our ports. Those
fortifications still stand, and they were once

the best of their kind. They are absolutely
·useless now, owing to the change and advance
in methods of attack, but they are nevertheless monuments of a well-settled American
policy and teach a lesson not to be neglected.

After our civil war the nation desired only
to rest and bind up its wounds. Navy and
coast defences were alike forgotten. At last
this neglect attracted public attention, and
under President Arthur and Secretary Chand-
ler we began to build a new navy. Somewhat
later we entered upon the reconstruction and
armament of our coast defences to suit modern
conditions. This renewal of our old and traditional policy went on with increasing vigor
until the foreign questions of the last few years
rose into prominence. Then it began to encounter opposition. The very people who
objected to our taking a firm stand in relation
to any foreign power, because we were defenceless and unable to resist attack, began to
oppose our taking any steps to put the country in a state of defence and able to resist an
enemy. This sounds like a paradox, and yet
the position is logical. The strongest card in
the hands of those who opposed the traditional American policy in regard to the Monroe Doctrine or Cuba, or anything else, was

in a desperate appeal to fear.   If the country's coasts were well defended and the American navy strong and efficient, they would be unable to make this appeal or to arouse terror, and so they went from the particular to the general and attacked the policy of building a navy or providing proper coast defences. Here again, as in the question of foreign relations, they departed widely from the past and took a line of action wholly new in our politics.

It is easy to see where the "jingoes" get their ideas of the proper foreign policy for the United States, and for the course which they advocate in regard to the navy and coast defences.   They offer nothing new and they do not seek war at all, but solely the preservation of conditions and policies which shall insure our peace and guard our rights.   They simply cling to the American traditions and beliefs which have been handed down to them from the time of Washington, and which all American statesmen have held to as articles of faith until these later days.   The interest of novelty lies with those who oppose these inherited and distinctively American policies and traditions.   What they offer as an advantage is not quite clear, but the danger of their proposed course is very obvious, for the nation that shrinks and yields is the nation which is sure to fight in the end when it is forced into it by neighbors whom their weakness has encouraged to attack them at a disadvantage.

·· The mission of the great American Democracy is peace. We seek no conquests and desire to interfere with no other people. But that mission can be fulfilled only on the condition that we show ourselves strong and not weak; firm and not vacillating. As we respect the rights of others, so must all others respect our rights, and the just control which we must exercise in the Americas.

THE END

ERRATA

Page 195, lines 13 and 14, for "Chabot" read "Chabot or Cabot"; line 22, for (chabots) read (chabots or cabots).

NOTE.—Chabot is the ordinary name of the fish used in Heraldry, but in the Island of Jersey there is a fish called locally "cabot."

www.ingramcontent.com/pod-product-compliance
Lightning Source LLC
Chambersburg PA
CBHW031332070726
47496CB00018B/1829